10|17

LP

PAI

Reckoning at Lansing's Ferry

Center Point
Large Print

Also by Lauran Paine and available from
Center Point Large Print:

Kansas Kid
Night of the Rustler's Moon
Wagon Train West
Iron Marshal
Six-Gun Crossroads
Prairie Town
Dead Man's Cañon
Lightning Strike
Tumbleweed Trail

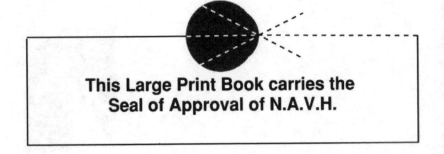

**This Large Print Book carries the
Seal of Approval of N.A.V.H.**

RECKONING at LANSING'S FERRY

Lauran Paine

CENTER POINT LARGE PRINT
THORNDIKE, MAINE

This Circle Ⓥ Western is published by
Center Point Large Print in the year 2017 in
co-operation with Golden West Literary Agency.

First Edition
October, 2017

Printed in the United States of America
on permanent paper.
Set in 16-point Times New Roman type.

ISBN: 978-1-68324-555-1

Library of Congress Cataloging-in-Publication Data

Names: Paine, Lauran, author.
Title: Reckoning at Lansing's ferry : a Circle V western /
    Lauran Paine.
Description: First edition. | Thorndike, Maine :
    Center Point Large Print, 2017.
Identifiers: LCCN 2017028034 | ISBN 9781683245551
    (hardcover : alk. paper)
Subjects: LCSH: Large type books. | GSAFD: Western stories.
Classification: LCC PS3566.A34 R43 2017 | DDC 813/.54—dc23
LC record available at https://lccn.loc.gov/2017028034

Reckoning at Lansing's Ferry

CHAPTER ONE

That empty plain ran on, wide and lonely and steeped in its own particular great depth of silence. Texas land in a great roll, spreading in seeming endlessness toward a dim merging with the vault of heaven. Where creek water flowed, one encountered plum thickets, willows, and cottonwoods, *bois d'art* from which the Comanches, who had formerly owned this land, had made their deadly bows and arrows.

This was the *Llano Estacado*—the Staked Plains—a wind-scourged emptiness in winter, a place of listlessness and orange-yellow sun smash in summer. But in the spring, which was settled now, the Staked Plains appeared as an Elysium with its brome grasses, its minute wild flowers standing straight in the profusion of rich forage, and with its fresh as water air and overhead pale blue sky.

In the Texas spring the Staked Plains were something to see. Hundreds of miles of good ground, greasy-fat wildlife standing sleek and sassy in belly-high grass, with the warm winds of Mexico holding sway and that winter cold from the north sheathed for half a year yet to come.

A good warmth lay over this monstrous land;

buffalo calves stood fresh born, wet and shaky, scenting the promise of life. Wild horses with matted manes and tufted snarls of winter hair sloughing off, flashed past full of the vigor that short, wiry forage provided. Overhead, heralding the arrival of this warm time of year, wild geese passed in clean and miraculous triangles calling down in their harsh and haunting way to the humans and the animals.

A few lodges of the *Teyuwit* Comanches were still to be found, hidden now from seeking eyes, or an occasional lodge of a *Ho'is* or Cross Timber Comanche, but generally this was an empty domain, an abandoned kingdom waiting with endless patience in good sunlight for its new masters to appear.

They came with the second-growth grass—the first growth was poor and watery. It weakened their animals and robbed them of vitality.

They came up from the south, driving wickedly horned, slab-sided, mean-eyed wild Texas cattle, a breed of lank and reckless men with the yeastiness of an uncertain future and a bloody past inherent in them. They came, mostly, fresh from their Lost Cause; fresh from the ragged ranks of a heroic Confederacy overwhelmed and vanquished, and they sat their Texas A-fork saddles believing stubbornly that they had not actually been defeated; believing instead—and it was largely true—that their Confederacy had worn itself out whipping an enemy who never stopped coming.

They pushed their herds on to the Staked Plains and took full advantage of the springtime richness which was abundant here. They threw down their bedrolls, chocked the wheels of their chuck wagons, set up rope and willow corrals, and for a little time rested while their animals fattened, gaining strength and stamina for the long drive yet ahead up out of Texas to the plains of Kansas.

And yet, as the Comanches had also clashed with foreigners in a fight to the finish for sovereignty of this grassland empire, the Texans crossed trails with an emigrant invader, too— settlers from the Yankee North. Union soldiers who had been rewarded by their victorious Federal Union with grants of free land. Texas land.

For a time, there was no open hostility. The Plains could accommodate all who came to populate them, but in the hearts of Texans lay a smoldering, a bitterness deep in the remembering blood. They passed those tent towns, those settlements along their waterways, those plowed plots in the heartland of their grazing domain, and they could not help but be struck by the difference existing between these newcomers and themselves. Differences not solely of origin, beliefs, attire, and bearing, but even of their common spoken language, and of their law, for at Phantom Hill and Pecos and Quanah, blue-belly Federal soldiers enforced the harsh edicts of a triumphant Union. Martial law existed, Yankee patrols scourged the land, and a Texan could do no right while a settler could do no wrong.

Ben Albright drove on to the plains with the warm winds of Mexico at his back. He came with six saddle-warped riders and a niece of his dead sister, pushing ahead of him two thousand dull red, two-year-old longhorn steers bound for Dodge City's booming beef market up in Kansas. Ben Albright knew the Staked Plains from the river Arkansas to the river Pecos. He had cursed gypsum drinking water from the Canadian to the Washita. He had driven over the white-oak bluffs to the chinaberry lowlands. He had savagely fought the Comanches, the killing blizzards, and the droughts. He had taken thousands of cattle up Pecos Valley, "graveyard of the cowman's hopes," and nothing had ever deviated unrelenting Ben Albright from the trail he had pioneered, and every mile of which was more familiar to him than the yard of his ranch back in Lipan County.

Ben Albright was a sere, lean, and dauntless fifty-five. He was tall and quiet-spoken and as deadly a man as had ever faced up to struggle and hardship. His eyes possessed that habitually drawn-out-narrow look of men accustomed to looking far out. His hair was grizzled gray and his mouth was a bloodless slit set across a blunt width of granite jaw. He had survived perilous times by adhering to a pair of cardinal virtues. Ben Albright never bluffed and he never threatened. He wore his guns as every man does who is familiar with their power and their finality. He had grown to manhood using guns. First, to provide himself with food. Then to protect himself and the things he believed in. And finally, to destroy those things that endangered the success of his enterprises. Ben Albright was a typical Texan of his times, and yet now, having passed the orders to his herd boss, Bass Templeton, to make camp there beside the sluggish Trinchera, Ben had another of those twinges of helplessness that had come to trouble him often during this drive.

He had never before taken a woman up the trail. In fact, he'd never heard of any other big drive being accompanied by a female, except for the Mexican girls, who sometimes went along with their particular cowboys. But this was entirely different. This was Atlanta Pierson, his niece, the daughter of his sister who had died on the eve of Ben's northward departure. There had been no one else to leave the girl with, and there had been no time to make arrangements to board her out.

Ben got down to stand in the warming sunlight at his horse's head, watching the herd fan out, scuffing dust up along Trinchera Creek, a tributary of the Río Grande. He saw how easily the men did their work, how routinely they took the mules off the chuck wagon, began making their lariat corral, threw down bedrolls and war bags, and off-saddled in the shade of the willows. He heard their musical calls rising over the duller sounds made by thirsty cattle. And he saw Atlanta sitting up there in her long, rust-colored riding skirt and full brown blouse, looking as fresh as though she had not just completed thirteen miles in the dusty drag pushing along the lagging and leg-weary longhorns.

At seventeen, Atlanta looked uncommonly as her mother had looked at that age, Ben thought. She had her mother's same great wealth of soft wavy black hair. The depthless dark eyes of gun-metal gray were also the same, and that wide, lush mouth with its ripe fullness, even to the faintly upcurving outer corners, was identical, too.

But Atlanta was taller than her mother had been. She was slightly larger at breast and hip, and there was a sturdiness to her, also, which Ben's sister had lacked. He had never known her father very well. Samuel Pierson had died in the Confederate triumph at Shiloh. But Ben thought now, for the hundredth time, that Atlanta's durability must have come from her father, because her mother had never been robust.

When Bass Templeton approached, spurs making soft music, Ben put aside these thoughts to listen to his herd boss' report.

"Camp's set up," stated Templeton, standing easy there, confident and calm in the face of his employer and their long-time association, the long length of him dusted and sweaty. "Ruben'll have supper ready directly. I'll go now and care for Miss Atlanta's horse."

"No," said Ben, glancing over where Atlanta had dismounted. She was stretching and spanking trail dust from her skirt. "She's seventeen, Bass . . . when my sister was seventeen, she was looking out for herself."

Templeton trailed his eyes over to the girl, balancing something in his mind but not quite up to saying it to Ben. He cast a long look out where the cowboys were drifting into the shade of the willows along the creek, for the time being free to relax. One of those men particularly caught and held Templeton's attention.

"That Case Hyle," he said eventually, then paused to fit the right words to his thoughts. "He knows the country . . . like he said when we hired him on back a ways. I've got a feeling about him."

Ben Albright looked outward for the man Templeton had referred to. He found him, not over in the shade but pacing along toward Atlanta with his rider's stride and his easy manners, clearly intent upon relieving the girl of caring for her horse.

"What kind of a feeling?" queried Ben, watching that tall silhouette stop close by Atlanta, thinking back to how Case Hyle had come riding alone into an evening camp sixty miles back asking for a rider's job, and how Hyle had impressed him with his quiet answers and his capable look. "He's good with stock," Ben said as much to himself as to Templeton. "He gets along with the men. He's not lazy around camp. What else do we have to know about a man, Bass?"

Templeton continued his onward gazing and said no more for a long time. A wisp of fire crackled down by their chuck wagon. Watery blue smoke stood straight up in this late afternoon's utter stillness.

Bass pulled off his gloves, poked them absently into his gun belt, and said: "Maybe it's just me. Anyway, I can't put my feeling about Hyle into words, rightly."

He started away and Ben brought his glance close in to follow Templeton as he progressed ahead toward the chuck wagon. He thought he knew what was in Bass's mind and it was in his own mind, also. Case Hyle always managed to be on hand when Atlanta's horse had to be cared for, or when she needed companionship, even when she was thirsty on the trail, or when she required

14

a screening rider to shield her from the dun dust.

But gallant manners were nothing to condemn a man for. Besides, Atlanta appeared in Ben's wise and knowing eyes to favor Bass over the stranger, anyway. Maybe a little jealousy might even inspire a little gallantry in Bass. There was room for that kind of improvement, Ben knew, for Bass had been going up the trail a long time now, and before he could hope to win Atlanta's full and acquiescing favor, he'd have to change from being a terse, rough, and bull-voiced herd boss.

What irritated Ben right then, as he turned to unsaddle, was the basic fact that Atlanta was along in the first place. A cattle drive was no place for a girl. It was hard work with long hours in the saddle. Men became lonely and restless. An innocent smile from Atlanta could very easily be misinterpreted.

Ben flung down his saddle, removed the bridle, and gave the horse an unnecessarily hard slap. He cursed and blew out a long breath. The last kind of trouble he needed on this drive was the kind that came with a beautiful girl in a land populated largely by lonely men.

He removed his hat, swiped sweat from the unnaturally pale skin of his forehead, tugged the hat back on again, and strode forward bound for the creek. Ahead at Lansing's Ferry there was an excellent chance of trouble. He walked now, thinking of this and pushing his concerns about his niece and other things from his mind.

For five years, the Albright herds had crossed their wagon at Lansing's. They'd re-provisioned at old Ewell Lansing's trading post, camped there a day or two, and had then gone on, swimming the cattle in that one still water, big pool where the Trinchera was least treacherous.

But old Ewell Lansing was dead now. Ben had been informed two months earlier, and others owned his ferry and trading post. Lansing's Ferry was now, in fact, a settler village of plowed fields, log homes a-building, mud-wattle soddies for those without the means for hauling logs from distant hills, and daily arrivals of new emigrants.

There had been some trouble, too. Jasper Higgins's herd had been turned away at the crossing. West Texans driving up the herd of Colonel Travis Bee had tangled with settlers and four men had died. The way Ben heard this, was that some of Bee's cattle had stampeded over a settler's melon patch, frightened by wash that was hung to dry from a wagon tongue and being whipped by a little wind. The settlers had gone to Colonel Bee's camp armed and in strong numbers demanding restitution. Travis Bee, Ben recalled from other days, had been a fiery, proud man, and when the smoke cleared, Bee and his herd boss were down dead, along with two of the Yankees.

Ben kneeled at the side of the creek, dropped his hat, and scooped up water. He sluiced dirt from his face. He filled his hat and trickled water over his head and down his neck inside his shirt until he felt refreshed. Then he eased back in the solitude of this little place, mottled with green willow shade, and lit a thin cigar. He would face tomorrow when tomorrow came. It had never been his habit to brood. He lived life for each of its separate moments, and, like most direct men, he found his greatest pleasure in the little things that made for each man the richness of his earthly existence.

He was still sitting there, quietly pensive, when Atlanta came along, carrying her hat, freshly scrubbed so that her golden flesh showed. She halted and smiled down at him, the darkness of her liquid gaze striking hard and deep down into Ben, reminding him of her mother.

"You look lonely," she said to her uncle.

He smoked on, comfortable and unchanging. "It's a good feeling," he told her. "In the evening of the day, as in the evening of a man's life, being alone lets the pattern of a man's recollections flow evenly with no single high moment standing out more than the lesser moments."

She dropped down beside him at the creekbank. He saw how her skirt drew taut at the hip curving where her strong thigh curved; how her blouse fell outward under strong pressure as she leaned there trailing a hand in the water. And how the reddening light of dying day deepened that healthy golden color of her smooth throat and lovely face. It did not seem possible to him that this was the same awkward child he'd visited between trail drives years before. It didn't seem the same because she had so thoroughly changed that he could not, for the life of him, find anything to say to her now. She might have been a stranger. In fact, he thought as he sat there, she *was* a stranger. He hadn't seen her in six years, before this drive. In that time, she had altered completely, and if seventeen seemed young and immature in his mind, this extraordinarily handsome young woman with him now, profiled so that he saw the rise and fall of her breasts, the knowing lilt of eye and lip, was anything but immature.

Ben let his cigar die out. They sat on, saying nothing, just relaxing and uncertain, each in the presence of the other.

CHAPTER TWO

From that camp at the Trinchera's creek-like southern estuary the Albright herd passed along northerly, following the waterway until its widening, deepening current began to hasten and murmur and show white-water rapids. Here, Ben knew, and said as much to Bass Templeton, it was likely they would meet the first settlers of the Lansing's Ferry village. He wanted the men to be especially alert here, particularly careful and prudent.

Here, too, Atlanta came along to ride stirrup-to-stirrup with her uncle, bringing to Albright's steady, hard gaze the flash and the pride each strong man feels and shows in his own way in the presence of a beautiful woman.

"Ruben told me about the trouble with the settlers yonder," she said. "I've been wondering why we had to trail this way, Uncle Ben?"

"I always have," he said. "It's our habit to cross the wagon here and re-provision with flour and what-not."

He put his gaze upon the wagon where it jolted along under Ruben Adams's hands. Ruben was Ben's own age. He was a crippled cowboy with all the ignorance, the superstitions, and the garrulousness of old Texas hands. He had been with Ben in the war, as had two of the other men on this drive—Bass Templeton and Ferdinand Haight. Except for this, Ben would never have put up with Ruben's constant nagging, his eternal meddling, and his annoying habit of secreting whiskey—and turning up gloriously drunk when they were a hundred miles from the nearest replacement for a cook. But Ruben was a fine camp cook, too. He could make sourdough biscuits in a wind storm and wild plum upside-down cake under circumstances that made simply boiling water a near impossibility.

"I suppose he told you of Bee's trouble there, and the way those people turned Higgins back."

"And," said Atlanta sweetly, "other things, too."

Ben snorted. "What other things? Ruben's a chronic gossip. He doesn't know any more about those people than you or I do, Atlanta. He hasn't been up here since he made the drive with me last spring."

He turned his head to look at his niece. He saw how she was considering him. He thought she was gazing upon him skeptically, wonderingly. It annoyed him, so he spurred ahead and called a pointless order to Templeton, then reined along until he was even with the new man, Case Hyle, on the far-right wing of the drive.

The land was beginning to buckle a little, to stand up from its eternal flatness in a series of lifts and rises. There was an occasional tree and, farther along, the ubiquitous mesquite, whose beans had furnished the Indians with food, and whose tough and wiry wood served Indians and whites alike with firewood. There were also mayhaws and red bark, ash and elm, and, still farther on, there was the swale that held Lansing's Ferry.

Here, topping out upon a rib of flinty soil, Ben had his first view of the crossing in something like a year. This view confirmed part of what he'd heard, too. There were close to thirty buildings down there, where before there had been only old Ewell Lansing's post, his barn, and his smithy. There were canvas tops down there as well, checked and scarred from the overland crossing, their huge wheels sunk-set in the springtime earth.

And there were people. He saw them standing clear of their homes and stores watching his flowing herd pour forth from the southern reaches, a rusty tide of red backs breaking for the creek-side shade and grass. He watched Bass Templeton loosely loping along to turn aside the foremost critters well away from the village's southernmost homes. He was surprised when a quiet voice spoke from behind him.

"If they've got whiskey down there, I reckon we'll do without a fit meal for another hundred miles."

Ben turned to consider Case Hyle sitting there, gloved hands lying easy upon his saddle horn, and he said: "If you got nothing better to do than talk, lope on down there and tell Bass to keep three men between the herd and the village until the critters settle down."

Hyle eased forward and went along without saying anything else or looking back. When he came to the leveled off area though, he slowed to a jog and looked back over his shoulder.

From where he watched, Ben could not see his expression, but there was something about Hyle's backward glance, his easy and calm riding stance in the saddle, that said very plainly he considered Ben Albright no more and no less a man than he himself was.

Ruben set up the wagon clear of the creek and began preparing the cooking fire. Bass Templeton positioned riders as Hyle had said Ben wished them placed. Ferdinand Haight, a thin and wiry man with a bubbling chuckle and a reckless eye, sat quietly giving stare for stare with the settlers who had come along to the plain beyond their village to stand and impassively consider this first Texas herd of the spring.

Ben watched all this from his little eminence. He saw Atlanta dismount over near Case Hyle and slap her leg with her hat. He saw how Bass rode close to the two, saying something to Hyle and then passing on. He saw the youngest of their crew, Will Johns, lean from the saddle to speak with a settler in a shaggy blanket coat and high boots. He kept his pale gaze upon these two as the settler raised an arm to gesture north and east, and, eventually, toward the south.

When this conversation ended and Will settled back, looking unconcerned, Ben shifted his attention to the herd itself. There was no danger of his longhorns going into that settlement. They were not homesteaders' critters that cried plaintively to be fed morning and night. They were not even cattle a man on foot could get within a quarter mile of. Ben had bought them from cane-bottom ranchers and others up along the Cimarron. They were more than half wild, and if they were approached, they would flee, but if they could not get away, they would drop their ugly long heads in a twinkling, paw once, and charge. They had survived this long by being competent fighters. They had scars upon them from peccaries, wolves, coyote packs, and cougars. They would molest a settler only if he first molested them.

Ben shook out his reins. Ruben's supper fire was merrily popping now and he had put up his sign to the riders. The men knew what this meant. It was if Ruben were saying: *Men, the creek is one hundred paces both ways. It takes water to make your coffee and clean up your dishes. If you want to eat, pick up a bucket on your way to the creek and fetch it back.*

Bass had gotten the cattle well away from Lansing's Ferry to the south and east. The riders were drifting in—all but the guard—to eat and rest a spell before alternating with one another on the night watch. In Ben's view, everything was as it should have been, except for those unmoving people at the outskirts of their village, watching the movement of the Texans and their herd. This did not trouble him, though, as he loped to the corral and turned out his horse. He was not a man who sought trouble and he had learned from many years of observing, that this also applied to most other people.

Atlanta came on to meet him, to turn and saunter back toward the chuck wagon with him. This time he said aloud what he'd noticed with some surprise other days on this drive.

"You never seem to get worn down, girl. I like that. Particularly in a woman."

"Haven't the women you've known, Uncle, been like that," she said right back, looking up into his face.

He reddened for no reason he knew of, and then he said: "It's uncommon in a female is all."

She let it die right there, for this obviously was his wish. Then she said: "Why don't you like Case Hyle?"

"What? Who said I didn't like him, girl? This here is a cattle drive. There's work to be done. If I am a mite short now and then, it's because

24

that's my way. But I don't dislike Hyle. If I did, believe me, I'd pay him off right here and now."

Atlanta walked another hundred paces before thoughtfully saying: "Uncle, will we move away from here tomorrow?"

"I expect," answered Ben. "After we buy a few things and have the wagon ferried across."

"Uncle?"

"Yes?"

"The settlers aren't going to sell us any provisions."

Ben turned half around and halted in a brusque manner. This was his habit for the facing of unpleasantness when it came abruptly. He put his dead-level pale gaze fully upon Atlanta as though she were a man, and he stood there without saying a word, just waiting.

"Will talked with their mayor," she explained. "He told me he said we'd get no supplies at Lansing's Ferry, and that the sooner we moved along the better his people would like it."

Ben listened to this carefully and turned it over in his assessing mind. Then he resumed his onward way again, sighting Ruben Adams at the supper fire and making for him in an unwavering line.

Bass Templeton and Ferdinand Haight were slouching up against a wagon wheel. They both watched Ben's thrusting long stride as he came up to the wagon. Then they exchanged a knowing look and bent to fill tin cups with black coffee from a battered graniteware pot, looking grave as they did so.

"Ruben."

Adams got upright and stood stiffly facing Ben. "Yes, sir," he said, his voice quick and nasal.

"Do you need supplies?" Ben asked.

Ruben looked past where Case Hyle and Will Johns stood back a distance. He saw Atlanta coming on slowly in her uncle's wake.

"Yes, sir," he said, shuttling his eyes back to Ben Albright. "We always provision here. Can't haul more'n 'nough flour and dried fruit in our one wagon to go much beyond Lansing's. You know that . . . sir."

Ben stood rock-like for a moment longer, then he removed his riders' gloves, pushed them into his belt, and stooped to take up a cup of coffee. No one said anything. Ben sipped and slowly turned to gaze ahead where the village was. Finally, looking at Johns, he said: "Will, just exactly what did that homesteader say to you?"

Johns was a youth in his late teens. He was normally an irrepressible spirit. He had come to Texas from Tennessee after the war like many another orphaned drifter, but the scars of a difficult early life did not seem, at this stage in his life, to be very deep, or likely to be very lasting. He was handsome in his boyish way, with unruly corn-colored hair and good features.

Now he was grave and careful, when he spoke, and uneasy under all those watching eyes.

"He come up to me, Mister Ben, and he said his name was Charles Connelly, and that he was mayor of that there town, and that him and his folks didn't want no Texas herds crossing over their land, and that they wouldn't ferry our wagon on over, and that they wouldn't have no truck with us at any of their stores."

Will Johns drew back a sweeping breath after getting all that out without stopping to take a breath. He shot a look to each in the group from beneath his curled hat brim and lowered his head self-consciously to examine something that was floating in his coffee cup.

Ruben Adams made a loud grunt, bobbed his head up and down, and resettled himself upon one knee at his cooking fire, muttering derogatory sentences under his breath and gazing with long-faced gloom at his cook pans.

Bass Templeton strode forward to dunk his empty cup in a bucket of water and hang by its handle from a bent wire. He carefully examined the backs of his hands and shot a speculating sidelong glance at Ben. Several times on this drive he had tried to talk to Ben about seeking a new way over the *Llano Estacado*, not that he had the least fear of homesteaders—he didn't have—but because he was a man with a mind that never lost sight of a goal, and the goal of an

Albright drive was now, and had always been, to get safely onto the Kansas plains with the cattle.

Bass knew how Ben felt. He had served with Ben under fire and he'd been up this same trail with him five times as well. Ben was being torn by the antagonism they all felt toward these Yankee newcomers, and he was also being plagued by his sense of duty, which was closely allied with something inherent in him. Ben Albright had never been backed down by a living man or a foreign principle. He could not, with any conscience, back down now.

CHAPTER THREE

The men all took their turns on the night watch, except for Ben and Atlanta. She had a pallet inside the wagon while her uncle and the others slept upon the ground not far from the dying cook fire.

There was rarely any visiting after supper on an Albright drive; the men were astride by five o'clock in the morning—four o'clock in summertime—and they worked through heat, storms, river crossings, stampedes, and hours of monotonous dust. When daylight ended and they had eaten, they ordinarily went straightaway off to their blankets.

This night was like most others; a little ripple of drowsy talk passed for a short time between those bedded-down riders. Then there was quiet. Ruben's fire dimmed down to cherry coals, and one by one these winked out, too.

Occasionally a steer bawled. There was a rustling sound along the creek where critters rubbed, or hooked willows in their horns, drew them carefully down, then walked out to their ends to eat the tender buds and leaves. A constant soft sound of animals at the water went on, and yonder a distance, where Lansing's Ferry lay, were orange pin pricks of lamplight and sounds of distant gaiety.

Dawn came early upon the springtime land. First was the pastel stain of diluted blue. Then a steady brightening pink. And finally a golden flash of light standing up from over the rind of the plain to dapple the high heavens with its silence and its fragile beauty.

Will Johns, who had the dawn watch, came jogging into camp where he got down slowly from his saddle, and pushed faggots into the buried coals of Ruben's fire. Like fireflies, sparks flew, followed by a pale tongue of flame. Will's face looked cherubic in this firming brightness. He briefly warmed his hands, looked around until he located Ruben Adams's sougans, and went over to push a spurred boot into the inert flesh there while quietly saying: "Ruben, your fire's lit. Dawn's here and daylight's comin'."

Adams blinked and sat up to expectorate. He never awakened feeling good and this morning was no exception. He called Will a name, then said: "You got to always kick folks up in the mornin', you damned Tennessee cotton-picker?"

Will hustled away, a smile on his face as he led his horse. Out where the corral was he stopped a moment to gaze ahead at Lansing's Ferry. He wished he might go down there. He'd wished he had that evening, before Ben had said they would all stay away from the settlers until he'd had a chance to talk to this Charles Connelly. Will's horse nickered. He wanted to be released to roll and drink at the creek and browse a little. Will began off-saddling. He saw nothing in that time of silence and stillness and he sensed nothing. Then his horse faintly snorted and rolled an eye. Will turned to look around, perplexed. He saw Case Hyle coming toward him from the creek, freshly washed and shirtless.

Will said: "You're up right early."

Hyle came on, saying nothing until he was close. Then he grinned. "When you're the first man stirring on drives like this, you get your pick of the saddle animals," he said as he began shrugging into his shirt.

He was a tall, broad man. Thirty years earlier, Ben Albright had looked the same. Hyle was flat; he had the hard angularity of men who made their living with saddles, horses, ropes, and cattle—and sometimes with guns as well. His flank was lean, his waist small, then his chest flared upward and outward into mighty shoulders. He was a smiling man full of poise and confidence and there was something else to him, too—an air of command, an aura of quiet and superior competence. Will felt it now, but, like Bass Templeton, he could not define it. It was just there, around Case Hyle, part of his moving and his breathing.

"Have you roused up old Ruben?" Hyle asked, without looking along to the cook fire.

"I did," said Will, turning his animal loose, "and like always he cussed me out."

Hyle chuckled. He had white teeth set evenly in the layered sun browning of his rather handsome face. He turned to put a gaze far out where the cattle were up and moving, some toward the creek, some farther out upon the plain in search of fresh grass.

"Sure wish we could ride into that little old town and ease off a mite before ridin' on," stated Will Johns. "Ruben says we won't hit no more towns until we're into Kansas . . . or near the border anyway."

Hyle considered Lansing's Ferry. It lay somnolent in the pale freshness of the new day. He shrugged. "Ben'll ride in. Maybe he'll take you along."

But Ben didn't suggest that later, when they were all eating by the chuck wagon. He leaned upon the tailgate, sipping the last of his coffee and weighing each of his men carefully from beneath his tilted hat brim. Then he gave out the morning's orders: "Bass, you and Case come along with me into town. The rest of you get camp struck and the cattle lined out to push over the creek. Ruben . . ."

"Yes sir, Mister Ben," said Ruben Adams in his quick, sharp voice.

"Hold the wagon by. If we strike some kind of an agreement, I'll send Case back for you. Then you can come on in and load up on supplies."

"Yes, sir. I'll be plumb ready and waiting."

Atlanta stepped around the far side of the wagon in a white blouse and fawn colored riding skirt. She was booted, spurred, and ready to ride.

The men smiled and seemed to come more alive in her presence, wishing her a good morning, one by one. Ruben took her coffee and food on the least dented of his tin plates. He seemed so entirely different from his usual morning self, smiling and eyes twinkling at the beautiful girl, that Ferdinand Haight and Bass Templeton, after exchanging a brief look, both chuckled quietly. Then Ben put his cup down, hard, and that briefly averted masculine attention swung instantly back to him.

Ben did not greet his niece, but when he was occupied with solemn thoughts, he never observed amenities, anyway.

"Bass, you and Case saddle up," he ordered. He had already rigged out his own animal. It stood behind him half asleep and waiting with a good saddle horse's endless patience. "Ferd, you and Will and Owen get the drive bunched along the creek. But don't cross it. Wait until I get back and give you the word."

When Bass and Case returned astride, Ben

stepped over leather and led out toward the village.

As the three of them passed around the rope corral, Ben said: "Listen to me now, you two. If those settlers are hostile, just remember we're in their town. I know how it is. They're damned Yanks. But the war's long over . . . and, anyway, we're way outnumbered. So, if they're of a mind to make trouble, don't forget we've got a spooky herd of wild two-year-olds." Ben paused before adding: "A stampede could cost us."

Ahead, in Lansing's Ferry, men came out into their roadway to stand facing south and watch the herd. Then these same men hastily broke up into little groups and faded out among the byways of the village.

Later, as Ben and Bass and Case were approaching the southernmost buildings, these same men accompanied by at least fifty others, all armed but not all fully attired, drifted clear of buildings and roadways to form a solid phalanx across their settlement.

"Well now," said Bass Templeton, drawing up a little. "Ben, I'd say those folks are plumb hostile."

Albright kept on riding, saying nothing. Case Hyle looped his reins, took out a tobacco sack, and began twisting up a smoke. He lit up, let the cigarette dangle from his lips, and slitted his eyes against the upcurling smoke. He was silent and watchful and looking speculative.

The same shaggy-bearded man who Ben had seen the day before speaking to Will Johns, wearing the same old blanket coat, moved out ahead of that silent, armed crowd of settlers, stopping to lean upon a U.S. Springfield arsenal rifle. He was not as tall as any of the three Texans, but he was easily as broad as the sturdiest of them. He had booted legs set wide and his shoulders pushed forward as though bracing into a high wind.

After Ben drew rein and nodded gravely to this man, he said: "You must be Mister Connelly."

"And you," said the bearded man in a rumbling tone, "would be Ben Albright."

"That's right. Now then, Mister Connelly, it's been my habit for some years to cross my wagon at Lansing's Ferry and to re-provision here. Old Lansing and I were close friends, and if you'll let me, I'd like to extend that same feeling toward you and your folks here. I've always paid the going price for victuals, and a dollar for crossing over my wagon."

Ben finished, anxious to hear Connelly's response. On his right, Bass Templeton was still and impassive. On his left sat Case Hyle, cigarette smoke trailing upward to break out and around his hat brim, pale eyes thinned out, and

35

both gloved hands lying crossed upon his saddle horn.

Charles Connelly eyed each of the three mounted Texans for a long while without saying anything. Behind him stood that crowd of unnaturally stiff and wary settlers, as quiet as night perching crows, and about as alike, too.

"I told your cowboy yesterday, Mister Albright," stated Connelly in his bull-bass and rumbling voice, "that we don't want any Texas herds driven through our settlement here. If we refuse to ferry wagons across and refuse to sell drovers supplies, I think in time you people will change your course and leave Lansing's Ferry alone."

Ben's reply to this was very soft, very cold. "Why don't you want drovers at your town, Mister Connelly? Is it because you don't care for Texans?"

"It's because," replied the burly, bearded man, his face hardening against Albright, "we aim to plow this land and put in crops, Mister Albright. We can't fence our land in because that would cost a lot of money. We have to spend our cash on seed and tools. If Texas herds pass this way, the cattle will just naturally trample over our grain and vegetables. It doesn't matter how careful you drovers are, that will happen and we can't afford for it to. That's the reason we won't have anything to do with trail herds." Connelly paused. Again, he studied the grim faces of all three horsemen in front of him. Then, in a hard tone, he said: "The fact that you are Texans hasn't a lot to do with it. I think we proved in the war that Texans are mortal. At least *I* think that, Mister Albright."

Bass Templeton turned slowly white down around the mouth. His eyes had in their deepest depths fire points of quickening anger. "If you'd care to step out from the protection of your men, I'm sure you and I . . . ," he stopped. Then: "God damn you, Mister Connelly, I'll . . ."

"Bass!" Ben's voice cracked.

The townsmen began to firm up over where they stood. Charles Connelly had his dark, sulphur gaze fixed steadily upon Templeton.

Ben Albright knew they had entered a bad moment, so he addressed Connelly in a voice loud enough for all to hear: "All right. I can understand your problem. Hereafter, my herds will detour around Lansing's Ferry. I think that is fair. In return, I ask that, this time, you cross my wagon and sell me provisions." He stopped, aimed a hard gaze at Connelly, and waited.

There was a faint murmuring from the line of townsmen behind the mayor of Lansing's Ferry. Charles Connelly twisted to gaze over at them. He came back around slowly and just as slowly shook his head. "We discussed this yesterday and last night, Mister Albright. It was the unanimous decision of our town council that regardless . . . we would ferry no drover wagons over the creek and we'd sell them no supplies." Connelly let this lie between the two groups over an interval of silence, before he concluded with: "We had trouble here last fall. Some men were killed. We aim to avoid that kind of thing now. We will not have anything to do with drovers at all, and that's final."

Ben's face turned smooth, turned iron-like. He continued to gaze upon the townsmen for a time, then he lifted his rein hand, spun his mount, and without a look at either Bass or Case, he went in a long lope back toward his creek-side camp.

The three of them got back to the wagon and stiffly dismounted. Bass Templeton and Ben Albright were white-faced angry. Case Hyle stood a little apart from them as Ruben and Atlanta came up, saw the look on Ben's face, and halted.

"Mister Ben . . . ," ventured Ruben, shuffling his feet.

"Get the men," Ben rasped to Templeton. "We'll cut willows and raft the wagon across." Then he turned back toward Ruben. "You cook without flour until we hit the border," he stated flatly, then dropped the reins of his horse and quickly walked away.

Atlanta gazed over at Case Hyle. "They weren't friendly?" she murmured.

"No, ma'am."

Atlanta looked thoughtful. She moved sideways to look down over the land toward the village. Where a thin line of men stood down there, well south of the buildings, other men, and even a few women, drifted up to stare toward the converging riders of Albright's camp.

"Case, they look as though they're armed," Atlanta said, and turned to gaze upward at Hyle. "Are they *that* hostile to us?"

"Yes'm. I guess they have their reasons. But all your uncle asked was the right to pass this one time. He said hereafter he'd detour."

"They refused?"

Hyle nodded.

Ruben Adams limped forward to glare at those watching townsmen. His lips moved jerkily but none of his words were audible. Then, back at the wagon, Ben bawled out for the cook, and Ruben gave a little hop and scuttled obediently away.

The silence where Case Hyle and Atlanta Pierson stood steadily deepened. Taciturn Owen Wallace, the only Albright rider who never appeared to be easy in the company of the others, came loping along. He was a swarthy man with exceptionally high cheek bones and a sloe-eyed black stare. He was strictly a loner; a man who seldom spoke, stayed to himself, and was so thoroughly unobtrusive the others rarely knew when he was close by at all.

Now, he stopped and tipped his head at Atlanta, then said to Hyle in his terse way of speaking: "No dice, huh?"

"No dice," repeated Case. "No crossing and no supplies."

Owen flicked his reins and looked ahead where the others were busy with the wagon. "He goin' to float it across?"

"Yes."

Owen eased forward in the saddle. "I wouldn't," he said as his horse began to move. "I'd burn their town and let 'em eat the ashes." Then Owen passed along.

Atlanta looked surprised at this. She watched Wallace's progress without saying anything, but her face showed troubled thoughts.

Case Hyle moved around her, murmuring— "Excuse me,"—and went along to add his considerable strength to the work ahead.

Floating their chuck wagon across the Trinchera was not really a dangerous or difficult undertaking. But Texan tempers were short as the men cut logs, lashed them to the wagon, and prepared to ease it down into the water.

Ben said to Case, as the latter came up: "You and Bass get on horseback and guide it across." He turned next to Will Johns and Ferdinand Haight. "You two strip down to your britches and swim with the damned thing. And Ruben?"

"Yes, sir, Mister Ben?"

"Get up in the wagon and make sure that whatever the water will spoil is piled high enough so that it won't get ruined."

Ruben turned his worried face, got up on the wagon, reminding his boss: "Mister Ben, I can't swim . . . remember?"

Case and Bass Templeton rode down into the creek and waited until the tongue had been lashed to the foremost wagon bow so that it would not drop down, strike creek bottom, and upset the wagon. Then, as the others got the rig moving, both riders eased forward with it. At once the creek's firm current made their animals brace hard.

Atlanta was watching from the shore. When Ferdinand Haight went into the creek, he gave a howl at its coldness. Atlanta smiled at this, but her uncle, who turned back at the last moment to run for his saddle animal, did not smile at all.

They got the wagon across and upon the far prairie without incident. The Trinchera's banks, like the banks of every waterway of the Staked Plains, was little more than a sandy sloping of earth to water's edge.

Ben called: "Atlanta, can you swim?"

"No, Uncle."

"Then get your horse and ride out into that creek, girl. You'll never learn any younger!"

CHAPTER FOUR

Owen Wallace stayed with the cattle. He rode quietly back and forth, preventing most of them from breaking away from the creek. The few cutbacks who headed around him did not go far. Texas cattle are gregarious. They do not like being alone and those cutbacks ran only a short distance before halting to throw up their horned heads and look down toward the water, and then they sidled close to the herd again.

Ruben got down from the wagon on the creek's far side and broadly smiled as Case Hyle dismounted to stamp water from his legs.

"I wasn't scairt," Ruben stated. "Not for myself anyway . . . just for the little flour we got left."

Hyle looked over. "Sure not," he said in a knowing way, and remounted.

Bass Templeton drifted over. He sat his horse stiffly watching Atlanta swim her mount across. He would have gone down to the girl but Ben Albright, upon the far shore, was sitting his saddle on a loose rein, watching Atlanta's progress also. It was very clear that Ben would, at the first inkling of trouble, jump his mount into the Trinchera to help his niece.

Atlanta's horse was a high-strung Kentucky animal. It lunged in powerful bounds and made the west bank, then stopped there to settle its legs and shake with great vigor. Atlanta was not nearly as wet as the men were. When she dismounted, she took off her boots and turned them upside down to rid them of any water. When she was done, she smiled over where Will Johns stood.

Roughly, Bass Templeton said aside to Case Hyle: "Come on . . . let's get the cattle." He then started riding back toward the water. As he passed Will and Ferdinand Haight, he said: "Hey, you boys, hang onto the tails of our horses and go back with us for your mounts."

Ben Albright was still sitting his horse across the creek. South of him the herd was spread out for over a mile along the creek, content there in the willow shade with good grass and water available. Northward was the settlement. Its people were darkening the plain below their village watching all this. A few were on horseback. Some of these were youths, and occasionally they would ride ahead for a closer view. They were all armed, these younger men, and they rode with an obvious insolence that made Ben consider them from a bleak face.

Case Hyle came up out of the water near Ben and started to say something, then he saw Albright's expression, locked down in wrathful hostility toward the settlement, and he swung his animal to ride south where the herd was. Behind him Ferdinand Haight and young Will Johns ran for their saddle animals while Bass Templeton drew up and halted at Ben's side.

"Everything's fine so far," Bass said, and waited.

Ben turned away from those cavorting riders, put his smoldering gaze on across the creek, then southward where Case and Owen Wallace were sitting in conversation, awaiting help with the herd. Ben didn't say a word; he simply swung his mount and headed for the cattle. Behind him came Ferdinand and Will, drenched but not particularly troubled for the morning's sun was increasing its warmth each passing moment.

"Take the point," said Ben to Bass Templeton. "When I wave my hat, ride on across."

Bass spurred ahead. He had done this dozens of times.

Ben looked to see that his other riders had taken their spaced positions on the herd's flanks. This was nothing new to any of them. They knew what to do and how it should be done. Ben sat on, running his smoky gaze up and down, then he flagged at Bass Templeton with his hat.

Bass rode slowly down into the water. This was a signal for the riders farther back to begin closing in on the rearmost critters. These, in turn, shouldered the animals ahead of them until this irresistible force built up solidly upon the reluctant cattle behind Bass.

These were the lead steers. They went down

into the Trinchera until little more than their high standing horns and shoulders showed, and began to swim. Behind them the balance of the herd came on. For a while it was difficult to see water at all, only a sea of shiny dark red hides accompanied by the sound of the clicking of horns.

The riders whooped and flagged with their arms and upheld coiled lariats. They gave the hesitant beasts no leeway for thought and in this manner nearly all the animals were forced into the creek. A few cutbacks panicked and turned around, heading in the direction from which they had been driven. Because longhorns customarily closed their eyes when charging, the cowboys made no frontal runs on these animals, but let them slow their furious rush, raise their heads, and look around. Then they rode wide around them, came in from behind, and started the process of easing these balky critters back toward the creek and their companions.

Will Johns and Case Hyle went after four of these cutbacks, got out around them, and were closing in, keeping their full attention upon the steers, when out of the east riding hard, came four youthful settlers who raised the yell and struck that little bunch of cattle, scattering them in wild panic in four different directions. Hyle reined back hard at this unaccustomed chousing and looked swiftly to see who these riders were.

Will, closer and therefore quicker to understand what had happened, let off an angry shout and jumped his horse straight into the path of one of those settlement men.

The settler's mount struck Johns's head-on. The impact of that collision was clearly audible over where Case was turning his horse to face the other three riders. Will and the settler went down, a great burst of dust jerked to life where the horses hit, and the other settlers hauled back in sliding stops to stare at that tangled scene of threshing animals and frantically moving men.

Case spun out in a run toward the dust cloud. Over the steady bawl of cattle, down by the creek, a man's quick shout echoed. Will Johns was on his feet first. He had lost his hat, and his shirt was torn from hip to shoulder. He stood briefly without moving, then hurled himself with a ripped-out roar upon the rising settler, struck this other youth as the settler was coming upright, and knocked him back down to his knees. The settler, still stunned from the collision, hung there on all fours, shaking his head, dazed. Will caught him by the shoulder, hauled him upright, and felled him with a sledging blow.

Case Hyle left his horse on the fly twenty feet away. He sprinted to get between Will Johns, who was furious, and the settler, who was awkwardly rolling over, scrabbling at the ground with numbed fingers, trying instinctively to regain his feet. He could not do it. He listed off to one side and fell back, wallowing in dust and making grunting sounds deep in his chest.

"That's enough!" shouted Hyle. "Will, get hold of yourself!"

Young Johns's face was a deep red from the fall. His gaze was glassy with hot wrath. "They deliberately spooked those critters," he rasped. "Case, didn't you see how they run on them cattle deliberately, tryin' to bust 'em like that?"

"I saw," answered Case, twisting a little at the sound of oncoming riders. "Now you slack off, boy."

The other three youths came up and halted to sit there, staring down at their groggy companion. One or two of them put their steady looks upon Will and Case. All the young settlers were armed. All looked furious.

Case said to them: "Don't make it any worse, fellows."

Onward from the creek came two loping horsemen. Sunlight flashed along a naked carbine barrel over the lap of one of the men. Case saw this and looked higher, at the face above that gun. These two were Ben Albright and dark Owen Wallace. Ben had the gun. His expression was like granite as he slowed to a walk and covered the last hundred feet in that gait.

Before Ben could speak, Case said to the settlers: "Get down and help your friend there.

Then go on back where you belong, and the next time you feel like trying to run off someone's cattle . . . *don't* do it."

Ben sat there glaring at the four teens from the settlement. A warning of danger was written on his face, in his terrible silence. His hand, which had remained curled about that Winchester saddle gun, was white with straining.

Will Johns went for his hat, struck dust from it, crushed it upon his head, and walked on to where his horse stood, to examine the animal for injuries. There were none, but the animal was shaking from head to tail with reaction to that powerful blow he had sustained. Will turned him several times, watching for a limp or a favoring of a leg, then he stepped over the saddle and sat back there, watching those settlers move forward to help their badly beaten companion to his feet and lead him away.

Case Hyle stood aside for a time, then turned to look down toward Lansing's Ferry. Men were beginning to gather into a group down there on horseback. For a time, Case watched this, then he moved to bring up the injured settler's horse. He stood at the animal's head while its owner was hoisted aboard. He waited before flinging the reins to another of the settlers. All this was accomplished in total silence.

Ben and Owen Wallace looked on, their expressions fierce and near to violence.

Case said to the settlers: "Go on now. And for their sake, I think you'd better turn back those men down there who look to be planning on riding out here." He made a short motion with one hand, then went along to his own mount, got astride it, and shortened the reins. He turned to Wallace, saying: "Owen, help me round up those damned steers." He did not acknowledge or speak to Ben at all. When he reined away, swarthy Owen Wallace rode with him.

The settlers walked their animals back toward Lansing's Ferry, holding in close to their dazed companion. Ahead of them, coming on at a stiff jog, were nearly two dozen other riders. Among these men rode Charles Connelly, the mayor, his bearded countenance and flapping blanket coat making identification easy.

Ben Albright sat on, watching this cavalcade swirl up around those other four riders. Behind him, from the creekbank, Bass Templeton and Ferdinand Haight came trotting forward and farther back. Across the creek, Ruben Adams ran up and down near where Atlanta sat her horse, patently perturbed by all this, but, because he had no saddled horse, unable to get back over the creek.

Most of the cattle were on the Trinchera's western bank. The few cutbacks, seeing this and motivated by that unique instinct longhorns

49

possessed, were mincing along the east bank, fretfully bawling.

Case and Owen Wallace had no trouble bunching those four critters the settlers had scattered, pushing them along to the creekbank, then forcing them into the water. They then rode up and down the creek repeating this process until the last of the Albright cattle were on their way to the west bank. Then they came together to sit in the protection of shade provided by the willows, looking out where Ben, Bass, and Ferdinand were talking to Will Johns.

Farther north were the mounted settlers. They had in part returned to Lansing's Ferry with that injured youth and his friends, but at least fifteen of them had not. These men, among them Charles Connelly, sat their animals in the morning's bitter yellow sunlight looking craggily ahead where the Texans also waited.

"I hope they open up," growled Owen Wallace. He cursed, then spat aside before adding: "I'd like to lead out through their dirty tent town . . . the damned Yankees."

Case said nothing. He sat there waiting to see what would ensue, but, as time passed, he became more solidly convinced there would be no more trouble. From experience, he knew it was the way of fighting men to either go into action at the drop of a word, a look, a curse, or, when these things did not trigger them, to stand stiff like strange dogs while their urge to combat dwindled.

This is what ultimately happened here. Connelly finally turned his horse and led out back toward Lansing's Ferry, and around him dutifully trailed his mounted band. Ben and his Texans also returned to creek side, after a time. They crossed over to the west bank and, without speaking, began to bunch the cattle for the onward drive.

Case parted from dark Owen Wallace to assist Ruben in hitching up. He saw Atlanta go past in a slow lope and he heard old Ruben's garrulous words without heeding them. He watched Atlanta swing in to ride at her uncle's side. He thought privately that if the girl knew men of Ben Albright's type better, she would leave him entirely alone for several hours yet. She would know that crusty Texas tempers did not diminish readily.

When Ruben was ready to drive on, Case got into his own saddle and ambled along to join the drag. But because their wet hides and good rest had invigorated the steers, there were at this early stage of the day's drive no hang-backs yet. So, Case looked far ahead where Ben and his niece were riding. He saw the girl suddenly rein back and turn aside to ride alone. He gently nodded his head. In time, she would learn about men like her uncle.

• • •

Lansing's Ferry dropped away. Midmorning advanced to near noon and dust hung above the drive. The Texans rode mechanically and the steers paced along in their same phlegmatic way, too. Ruben's wagon creaked along through the flatlands. It was hot. They were without cover and after the water dried from their clothing, that burning sun that was upon them kept up its bitter punishment. Albright's longhorns raised dust in dun clouds, making the men cough and the horses repeatedly blow out through their noses.

Bass Templeton, in his traditional place far ahead at the point, looked back often. He did not seem, in Case Hyle's eyes, to do this with the cattle in mind, for each time his gaze sought out and briefly held to Atlanta Pierson.

Ben Albright rode easy in the saddle, a stiffness gradually leaving his shoulder points, his head beginning after a long time to swing casually right and left as he ran out his experienced look at the cattle.

There was no water and by early afternoon this became the source of bawling among the steers. Ben loped ahead to speak briefly with Templeton, and afterward Bass ran on ahead while Ben took his position at the lead point.

For another hour, they crawled over the heartland of this huge land dwarfed to ant-size by an overhead endless brassy sky, as well as by

52

the timelessness of this place where a day was only the merging of dawn with hot midday, and the dwindling of that scalding heat into watery evening. Then Bass appeared far out, dwarfed to insignificance, standing upon the ground in the meager shade of his saddle animal.

As the lead came up, Bass flagged with an upflung arm toward the shimmering east. He had found where the Trinchera curved away from Lansing's Ferry again, and was now motioning the herd in this new direction—toward water.

Another hour passed. The cattle scented the water. So did the saddle animals. There came to the pace of all these beasts a new vigor, a fresh and anticipatory springiness. Case felt it in his own beast. He also noticed that the drag critters were no longer shuffling along with that bovine listlessness that turned the most belligerent longhorn into an indifferent shambling hulk.

The sun slowly went lower, laying a sullen red glow over the plain, hurting the eyes of the Texans until they came to the end of the tame prairie and encountered once more that tangled wilderness of the Trinchera's creek sides, only up here where no settlers had thinned that profuse undergrowth, despite the relief of shade, thorn pins brought blood more than once to men and animals alike.

CHAPTER FIVE

They watered the herd in midafternoon and hazed it along until pre-evening's saffron glow gilded the land with a soft-shining obscurity, then Ben passed word along that they would make the night's camp. At once Ruben blocked his wheels, turned loose his harness horses, and set to work preparing the evening meal.

Atlanta passed Bass Templeton on her way to the creek, tilted him a smile, and passed beyond sight where wild grapes grew.

Will and Ferdinand stayed with the herd until Ruben beat the bottom of a pan, which was the supper call, then loped out and around the spreading critters and on toward Ruben's cooking fire smoke that stood straight up.

Ben rode toward the campfire, too, but in an angling way so that he intercepted Case Hyle a quarter mile out upon the plain.

When they came together, Ben said: "You did well back there today." His meaning was clear enough. "It could have ended like it did for Colonel Bee."

They rode on together, Case saying nothing and Ben pensive and seeming tired. "But it won't go so well with the next herd through here, Case. Those young bucks were full of arrogance. That happens when you let people turn you aside. Some of them, mostly the young men, right away think they've beaten you some way. They get full of pride."

Case looked around at the older man. "Maybe," he murmured. After a brief pause he added in a stronger voice: "But maybe Connelly's smarter than he looks. If he is, he won't start a war down here where he's outnumbered by Texans a hundred to one."

"Ahhh!" exclaimed Ben Albright. "You're forgetting . . . this is Reconstruction. Connelly's kind has the blue-belly troops on their side. Texas is still an enemy state . . . she's not back in the Union yet. The Connellys here have their arrogance . . . and their Union Army." Ben plucked off his gloves as they approached camp. "But, anyway, you did well today," he repeated, and this was as close to a compliment as Ben Albright ever came.

He loped ahead to put up his horse.

Case dismounted near Bass Templeton to say: "Who draws the first night watch?"

Templeton replied without looking around: "Will. Then Ferd and Owen. Last, will be you and me. I'll take the pre-dawn. You'll take the dawn." Then Templeton turned and walked away.

Atlanta, who was yonder by the wagon, saw this. She also saw the long, considering look Case put upon Templeton after he walked out to the corral. A little cloudy, troubled look came to her face. Then Ben strode up to speak to her and she did not see Case again until later, when he'd returned from the creek, freshly scrubbed, and came along to take up a tin plate and eat. By then Bass was also eating, sitting cross-legged near the fire, and seemingly that little incident was quite forgotten.

Ruben seemed fidgety this night. He moved with more than his customary jerkiness and there was an urgency to him that Case and Atlanta both noticed. When Will went away and returned without water, Ruben scolded him. Young Will stood there impassively with his clear gaze upon the older man, then he took up a bucket and wordlessly went to the creek.

Afterward, he sank down beside Case and said in a strong whisper: "Someday I'm going to up-end that cussed old mossy-back and dunk him in one of those buckets of water."

Ben made a cigarette when he'd finished eating. He smoked it, considering first the high, grand sweep of dark overhead sky. Then he stood, looked south-eastward, back where Lansing's Ferry was, and for a long time in his silent way he smoked and stood like that.

Bass put aside his plate, and reminded the men of the order of their watch. He got upright stiffly and passed along to Atlanta's side, leaned there upon the wagon's rough front wheel, and made a smoke.

After standing there silently for several minutes, he said to Atlanta loud enough for the others to hear: "The nights up here are about as fine as a person ever sees."

Atlanta nodded and smiled, but she did not speak. She went on eating her supper.

Ruben's agitation appeared to increase as the men took their plates to a bucket, carelessly sluiced them off and placed them upon the chained-up tailgate before drifting along, idly smoking, thoughtlessly talking, and heading for their sougans. Ruben waited until Ben walked clear, then he clambered over the tailgate, and was gone nearly a full minute. When he came scuttling back out again his cheeks were splendidly rosy, his faded eyes glistened with expansive amiability, and his breath reeked of stout rye whiskey.

The soft night's lingering last paleness winked out. The heat remained, pulsing upward from the baked earth, and where sap ran among the trees and vines at creek side, there was a musty fragrance that was not unpleasant at all.

Ben Albright was uneasy this night. He lay upon his ground sheet feeling tension in the roundabout gloom. He finished the cigarette he'd made after supper, stubbed it out, and raised up to look over the camp. Ruben alone remained by the fire, everyone else was away in darkness. A little fiery tip glowed and then dulled out over where Bass Templeton's bedroll lay. Bass, Ben thought, perhaps also felt that indefinable cross-current of impending events. He was not asleep.

In fact, Bass was sitting upright on his sougans faintly etched by Ruben's diminishing little fire, looking for all the world like a Comanche medicine man. His face was darkly limned and moody. His narrowed glance was directed ahead where the willows and cottonwoods were thickest. He smoked without moving, all his attention obviously down upon something there in those yonder trees.

Ben dropped back down. He had not seen Case Hyle and his niece strolling the hot, bland night toward the west bank of the creek. He thought only that he and Bass Templeton were being troubled by the same elusive worry. Ben put aside his hat, turned up onto his side, and closed his eyes. Whatever was coming would come, and he would face it then, but not until then.

Where the Trinchera's north-to-south swift passing cut at a cottonwood's dead bole it made a softly sucking sound. That lap of water was like light music in the warm night. Nearby lay the corpse-gray trunk of a cottonwood that had fallen to earth in decades gone, its bark sloughing off to present only the smooth underside of fine-grained wood, bone dry now and as hard as oak.

Over the plain itself there was a total stillness, which was unusual. Two thousand Texas steers did not very often all bed down simultaneously. This night though, they had. The silence was complete, except there by that deadfall cotton-wood. The night's great mystery lay on all sides. Above, stars flashed their diamond-like glow in a purple setting of moonless heavens.

Case Hyle was conscious of the rhythm of Atlanta's body as she strolled through all this pleasantness beside him as far as that deadfall cottonwood. There she paused to look skyward, then along the faintly lighted Trinchera waterway. She stepped forward to turn and seat herself upon that old fallen tree and then gazed up at Case, her expression made soft, made sweet by the night, and by her gentle thoughts.

After a length of quiet meditation, Atlanta said: "I watched you this morning . . . with those men from that settlement, Case. You handled that very well. But I had a feeling then, about you. You aren't like the others. There is a difference. I'm sure my uncle and Bass have noticed this, too."

He leaned upon a tree regarding her. His expression was thoughtful. "No two men are alike," he said. "There is always a difference. You discovered that today, I think."

"What do you mean?" she asked, genuinely puzzled.

"When you went up to ride with your uncle

after we'd lined out the drive on the west bank. I watched you, Atlanta."

She looked swiftly away from him, responding quietly: "Yes, I understand now. I should have stayed away from him."

"For some men, it takes a while for their temper to cool. Your uncle is that kind of a man."

"And you, Case . . . what kind of a man are you?"

He didn't answer her directly, but said in a fading tone: "Sometimes like your uncle. Sometimes not."

She arose from the log, made a quarter turn, and halted close to him. Star shine threw its filtered light across her face. He saw its flawlessness, its beauty, and he also saw unknown things deep in her eyes.

"Tell me about yourself," she said, and this was not a woman's curiosity. It was the kind of interest only a woman felt who was sincere in her wish to know about a particular man.

"There's not a lot to tell, Atlanta. I'm a Texan. I grew up beside the Río Grande. I still have kin down there . . . but I haven't seen them in many years."

"You were in the war?" she asked softly, hesitating as she watched the willow shadows move across his face.

He raised his head at this, put his steady gaze fully upon her and seemed to be carefully

60

considering what he would say next. "Yes, I was in the war." He straightened up off the tree at his back. "Did you know," he went on very quietly, "that Texas furnished one regiment and nine companies of cavalry to the Union?"

She stiffened slowly under his stare.

"And that Alabama furnished one regiment and five companies. That Arkansas sent seven regiments. That Mississippi sent north a full battalion. That Louisiana sent five regiments . . ."

He said all this in an impersonal manner, as though it were a page out of history that didn't much matter now. It showed his strong streak of fatalism. It made him seem older than he actually was. She felt all these things even while what he was indirectly saying to her slowly sank in.

"Case," she murmured. "You're saying, I think, that you fought *against* my uncle, and the others. That you fought with the Yankee Army."

"Yes'm."

She stood still and silent for a long while. Then she went back to her deadfall cottonwood and weakly dropped down again. "The others don't know that," she said, making a statement of it. "My uncle would fire you tomorrow . . . on the spot . . . if he knew."

"I reckon so, Atlanta. You can tell them, if you're of a mind to."

He moved over to her. Stood beside the fallen old cottonwood watching her face.

She swung to face him, looking very troubled.

"No. If I told them . . . ," she began, but stopped.

"A man does in life what he believes is right," said Hyle, interrupting her, bending a little toward her. "I believed in a solid Union. I knew a lot of other Southerners who felt the same way. I was there when some of them were killed, Atlanta." He put forth a hand, let it rest lightly upon her shoulder, before continuing. "This is not an easy thing to discuss though. Not tonight." He stepped back bringing her upright off the log with that compelling hand upon her shoulder. He drew her in close, saying: "The curse follows a man forever, I reckon, when he stands up for what he believes in. In the North, I'm a Texan. In the South, those who know, call me a traitor."

He let that restraining hand drop away. Around them night's warmth and strangeness ran on. Closer, they stood together feeling the same confusing, the same troubled emotions. He looked down into her face with that unique slanting expression she'd seen him use before, which was so near smiling and so near irony.

"If I was your uncle," he said next, "I'd say to you . . . 'Atlanta, hate a man who wrongs you, admire a man who believes as you believe . . . but respect with your whole heart the man who knowingly faces ostracism and stands forth for the things he sincerely believes in.' "

He dropped his shoulders a little, lowered his head, and cut out the night with the broad brim of his hat as he sought, and found, her parted lips with his own mouth. He stood without otherwise touching her for a long moment, then gently drew away. He stood back, unsmiling, looking down into the misty depth of her eyes, seeing them blacker than they normally were and filling with quick, stinging tears. He took her hand in his, turned, and started back toward camp.

"Come along," he said, as though she were ten years old. "Dawn will be here soon enough."

He stopped once, as they came clear of the thicket, smiled at her crookedly, and said: "Good night, Atlanta. I didn't do that to see if I could." Then he bowed and walked on.

CHAPTER SIX

Ruben had made several excursions to his secret place in the chuck wagon. Each time he came back to the fire though, he sat with his back pleasurably leaning against a high wheel and stared into the coals. When these died, he put on more faggots and let them die also. He did this the whole night long and only once did some of his usual irascibility show. That was when Owen Wallace began to snore in a bubbling way. But Ruben did not go over and rouse the sleeping cowboy, for of all the men on this drive he was most uneasy around Owen Wallace.

So he sat on, pleasantly glowing, alternating between dropping off and blinking awake. He heard Will come in from the plain and rouse Ferdinand Haight. Later, he saw Ferd come in and Owen go out to take his place riding around and around the bedded cattle. And still later, when Ruben was beginning to get really drowsy, he saw Bass rise up long before it was time for him to go relieve Owen, make a smoke, and sit there smoking, his face bitter as he inhaled. He saw Bass glance toward the wagon, and after that run his eyes along the ground to where Case Hyle slept.

Bass was ready to ride long before Owen

Wallace came in. He took his saddled horse with him to the cook fire and got a cup of black coffee. That was when Bass saw Ruben sitting there, watching him.

"What the hell?" he said, astonished. "How come you're up so early?"

Ruben made an impish smile and pursed his wet lips in a secretive way. He did not answer.

Bass sipped and gazed downward. He lowered the cup, stepped over closer, and bent down. "Well, I'll be damned," he exclaimed quietly, straightening back up. "Ruben, you've been drinking again."

Ruben's smile faded. His leathery old range riders' cheeks showed Bass nothing but a settled melancholy. He still said nothing. He did not wish to speak. Also, at that particular moment, he did not like Bass Templeton, either. He was certain Bass would tell Ben Albright about this, and the sparks would fly again.

Bass swished his coffee dregs and remained a while longer, watching old Ruben. Out where the rope corral was, horses stomped the hard-packed earth, crunched their teeth over willow shoots, and milled expectantly with the coming of dawn.

Bass said: "Ruben, you give me half an hour to get out with the herd, then you wake Case Hyle and send him out there to me."

Ruben looked up. There was something feline, something sly and scheming in Templeton's face.

"All right," Ruben replied, and afterward watched Bass mount up and rein clear of the camp in a slow walk westward. Something, Ruben told himself, is shaping up here. Something is building up between those two. He bent over to get himself a cup of coffee. It was hot and bitter and it had a disgustingly sobering effect upon him almost at once. He made a face and threw the dregs into the fire. A hissing arose accompanied by steam. Ruben nodded wisely at this, saying aloud: "You see, god-dammit . . . that stuff'll even kill a fire." Then he fumbled for his tobacco sack and made a cigarette. He would have just time for this before his day's work began.

From inside the wagon, he heard Atlanta turn on her pallet. A little moan escaped her.

Ruben looked solemnly at his cigarette, mumbling to it: "That's how it is, my friend. I seen 'em walk together last night, and that's how it is with 'em at their age. It hits 'em hard and it hurts worse'n a stab wound." He shook the cigarette and frowned at it. "Don't you tell me I don't know, consarn you. I know all right. Memories may be ashes in a man's heart but they're always there." He threw down the cigarette, stamped upon it fiercely, and pushed himself upright, flinching from a hot pain in his bad leg, and, teetering there, looking beyond his fire for the bedroll of Case Hyle. Then he started toward it, limping as he moved.

Case Hyle, Ruben discovered, was an inordinately light sleeper. Ruben had barely reached out his hand to nudge Hyle when, in a split second, a six-gun barrel was whipped up to halt inches from the cook's face. Ruben's breathing hung up; he froze there on his haunches.

Then Hyle lowered the gun and sat up. He said, as though nothing had happened: "Time for me to go relieve Bass?" Then, with clearing vision, he looked in a mildly puzzled way at Ruben. "How come you to wake me instead of Templeton?"

Ruben was breathing again. He rocked back on his heels and looked indignant. "What the hell you point that gun at me for?" he demanded indignantly. "All I was tryin' to do . . ."

"Habit," Hyle explained, pushing back his blankets and springing up. "I apologize, Ruben. I learned to sleep like a cat during the war. It was just habit."

Hyle smiled. He was a handsome man and his smile had a good effect upon people. He patted Ruben's shoulder and scooped up his hat.

He was rolling his sougans with his back to the cook when Ruben, entirely mollified, said: "Listen, Case . . . Bass told me to waken you and send you out to him at the herd."

Hyle made the final lashing on his blankets and looked around. "Something wrong?" he asked.

Ruben ran a hand along his bristly jaw. He squinted at the slumbering camp around them, then he lowered his voice to a whisper: "Pardner, he's goin' to tear you limb from limb."

Hyle said nothing but he was considering Ruben in a careful way. The humor, the easy poise, and the comradeship was completely gone from his face now.

Ruben was reminded of Ben Albright the way Hyle stood there waiting for an explanation. Ben had that identical way about him.

"Case, I dunno 'bout this, but I think he saw you and Miss Atlanta walk down by the creek last night."

"What's wrong with that?"

Ruben squinted. "Don't you remember him askin' her to go walkin' and her not answerin' him?"

"No," said Case. "I don't remember that at all."

"Well, maybe he didn't ask her in so many words, but he went over to her at supper last night and said what a bee-utiful night it was . . . and all."

Case recalled that incident all right, but he had not then thought much of it. "You're putting meaning into something where I don't think any such meaning was intended," he told the cook.

Ruben turned sly and knowing in his expression. "Case, you don't know Bass like I do. I been up this consarned trail with him a good many times. He don't say anything he don't mean to say. Bass don't make any idle talk . . . ever. He meant that exactly the way I just told you. She didn't go walkin' with him but she did go walkin' with you. Now he's out there burnin' up inside and waitin' to beat you to a pulp." Ruben inclined his head. "You deserved a warnin' and now you've had it."

Ruben turned and walked away. He only went as far as the wagon's far side. There, he swiftly turned and peeked out to watch Case get a horse, saddle up, and ride in a stiff jog out into the pre-dawn, star-showered silence. Then Ruben went sprinting after him in a crabbed way, face bright with anticipation, entirely forgetting it was time for him to start breakfast.

Albright's steers were grunting up out of their beds and beginning to browse. There was a good coolness to this small hour time of dark morning. Off in the dim east the earth's far crust was beginning to loom solid against a very faint brightening.

Case rode slowly in a northerly direction to the farthest extremity of the herd, then began the customary encircling movement that took each night hawk around and around those two thousand animals. When he was a mile out, a little red glow of flame showed where Bass Templeton sat his horse, smoking. Case made for that spot and saw Templeton lift his head and swing it quickly at the sound of his coming. Case went on, then drew rein fifty feet off.

"Bass, I understand you want to see me," he said.

Ruben, near out of breath from hurrying, heard this. He also heard Templeton's heavy answer.

"Yeah. I want to give you a chance to change your ways."

"All right," came Hyle's quiet reply to this. "Go on."

"Stay away from Ben's niece, Hyle. Stay plumb away from her."

Case sat his saddle for a moment after Bass said this, then he swung out and down. He walked to the head of his animal, holding the reins in his hands, and looked up at Bass. "I don't think you mean that," he said. "I don't think you're that unreasonable, Bass."

Templeton unloaded in a quick rush. He balanced forward on his toes. There was a fierce brightness in his hazel eyes, and Case knew in that savage second just how correct old Ruben had been. Shock went through him. It was a raw flash of warning striking every nerve and leaving him feeling entirely cold and loose in every inch of his body.

Templeton said hoarsely: "I've had all night to think this out, Hyle. I saw you two go walking. Now I'm giving you one second to make up your mind."

Something ancient and primeval stirred in Case Hyle. He knew what Templeton meant to do. It was like a silent message passing from Bass to him. He let go his horse's reins and stood there, hearing the abruptly increased sloshing of his heart in its dark cage. Templeton stood out very clear to him now, for some mysterious reason. He could see every deeply scored line around those flaming eyes.

"My mind's made up," said Case, his tone soft, his way of speaking quick and strikingly hard in the stillness. "If there's to be a choice made, why I reckon it'll be up to Atlanta to make it."

Templeton's feet were dug in. He launched himself forward like a catapult, swinging and grunting from this effort. His big hand grazed Hyle's cheek upward, knocking off his hat and sliding through his hair. Hyle jumped back and threw a punch that missed as Templeton rushed past, came heavily around, and lowered his head to charge again.

Maybe thirty feet out, where Ruben Adams had stationed himself, the camp cook was suddenly stone sober and still.

He danced and threw lefts and rights and pirouetted away from an imaginary foe. He grunted and winced when one of the blows made by Case or Bass connected. He gasped when Case Hyle dropped an overhand sledging blow to

Bass Templeton's neck. And he groaned through locked teeth when Templeton caught Hyle a solid slam in the belly.

Case danced clear after that blow, gulping air. Bass came after him with his long reaching arm. Hyle beat this strike aside and continued to back-pedal. Bass's next blow was aimed better and he was closer; it ripped through Hyle's hasty guard and cracked along his jaw. Hyle's arms nearly dropped. His head snapped from the impact and he tried instinctively to jump clear. He was only partially successful. There was a steady roaring in his head.

Templeton bored in, big arms working like pistons, hard fists sinking into meat to their wrists, each strike making a sodden sound. Hyle turned to absorb this punishment along one side, then he whipped up two short punches, both connected, and Templeton went back a little, off balance, and grunted. Hyle still back-pedaled, waiting for his vision to clear.

Bass rocked a moment with both arms down, peering out at his enemy. Then he came on once more in that same mauling lunge, arms up and pumping. This time Case let him come.

Ruben, closer now and breathlessly watching, turned stiff all over, straining forward, as those two big men met head-on, both forward on their toes, heads down, throwing everything they had into the fight.

The meaty sound of those terrible punches made shock waves in the softly brightening atmosphere. Templeton dropped his head, got both shoulders down behind his blows, and teetered there, slugging. Case Hyle's fists lashed in and out, then upward to Bass's face. One of these blows squarely connected, staggering Templeton back. But the herd boss held to it, his strikes as punishing as the downsweep of a splitting wedge.

Case then took one sideways, sidling step, and when Templeton twisted to adjust to this, a fist came out of the night to crack across Templeton's jaw. This time Bass's arms went fully down and his knees buckled. He rolled his head, escaping the follow-up to this hurting punch, and rode out the terrific beating that ensued. Then he lunged, caught Case full on in the middle, and both men hung there rasping for breath, battered and bruised and bleeding.

Ruben thought it was over. That it had ended in a draw. He was straightening up out of his own crouch when Templeton ripped out an oath and hurled himself upon Case Hyle. He had the momentum for this onslaught, but he no longer had the power to follow it up. When he threw a fist, Case blocked it and countered with two short, stinging rights. Bass gasped a bubbling breath and dropped back.

Case went after him and Ruben was dumbfounded. Hyle had been feigning that exhaustion. He pressed in, got against Templeton, and battered his midsection pitilessly. Then he shifted, struck Templeton high in the chest, and followed him when Bass staggered from this blow. He kept following him with both arms working. Templeton gave ground, his breath sawed in and out, he was taking a terrible beating and could no longer summon the strength to defend himself. Case's strikes were wicked. They were savagely effective, but stubborn Bass Templeton would not go down.

He wobbled and hung there and took that punishment. Case stepped clear, measured Bass for a final blow just as the herd boss' knees began to bend. His shoulder down, his bleeding fist cocked, Case gradually came up out of his crouch, gradually lowered his arm as he looked into Templeton's face. Then he put forth a tapping set of knuckles, rapped Bass's chest with them gently, just before the herd boss slid down in a heap, spreading out his full length in the churned prairie earth.

It was all over.

Ruben had seen all this, had lived it and felt it. He watched Hyle walk over to his horse, throw both arms over the saddle, and drop his head. Ruben gazed at the still, beaten form of Templeton, then he gave a jump. From back at the camp the unmistakable loud and indignant voice of Ben Albright was calling profanely for Ruben and his breakfast. Ruben gasped, spun about, and went in his crippled run back toward the wagon.

CHAPTER SEVEN

Case Hyle got Bass Templeton as far as the creek and left him there, his horse tied nearby in some willows. Afterward, he returned to the herd, feeling no desire for breakfast, at all.

He rode out as far as a little stubby knoll, dismounted up there, and gravely made and smoked a cigarette. He had washed at the creek but his bruises, if anything, looked worse after that cleansing. He sat near his horse, working the knuckles of his hands to prevent stiffness, and was still doing this when the sun came jumping out of the distant east. Simultaneously with this, a rider came loping forward around the herd toward his little knoll. Case smoked and watched this moving shape, and wondered what he should say when he determined that it was Ben Albright.

By this time, Case knew, Templeton would be back in camp, the others would be preparing to move the herd out, and among people with even the slightest powers of observation, it would be no secret that he and Templeton had fought.

Case did not know yet about Ruben. He could not therefore appreciate that Ben Albright and the others had been held breathless while the cook had given a graphically pantomimed and verbal description of that epic battle long before; even before Bass came riding in, looking as though he'd been attacked by a meat grinder. Nor could he know that the others back in camp, including Atlanta, had surmised the cause of that fight, and that each of them, according to his or her own private convictions, was now reacting accordingly as they saddled up to begin this new day's work.

Albright slowed his horse at the foot of Case's little hill, put the beast to it, and climbed the slope. When his animal halted, slightly puffing, Ben got down and came forward. Before he spoke, or even put his keen glance upon Hyle though, he turned and for a long moment stood there gazing out and down at his herd of longhorns. Then, still with his back to Case, he said: "On cattle drives it's always the unexpected that a fellow should expect, isn't it?"

Hyle did not answer. He got to his feet and leaned against his horse.

Albright turned, studied Case's battered face, and looked thoughtful. "I figured I could count on you two to show judgment," he stated. "But then I knew if I brought Atlanta along this might happen. I reckon it's more my fault than yours."

"He'd been eating his heart out," Case said finally, speaking softly. "I didn't know that."

"No, I expect none of us did. I should've suspected it if anyone should have. I've known

Bass a long time. He's an inward man sometimes . . . with things that are close to him, anyway."

"Of course, I'll have to draw my time now," Case said.

Ben stood easy and loose. His frosty gaze was undecided and that bright yellow sun rising was turning his cheeks their accustomed dull bronze. He slowly drew forth a cigar, lit it, and scowled through the billow of smoke he made. He studied Case Hyle for a long time before saying: "That'll be up to you, young man. I won't fire you, if that's what's in your mind. These things happen, and given enough time they work themselves out." Albright kept his gaze upon Case when he was finished. He was clearly trying to see beyond Hyle's melancholy expression to the secret thoughts beyond.

"I'll tell you one thing, though," Ben said, having decided to continue. "If you choose to go on with the drive, I'll not meddle. And another thing . . . since you beat Bass fair and square, he won't be your mortal enemy. You can trust him to face you any time that becomes necessary."

"Did he say I beat him fair and square?"

"No. Ruben said that."

"Ruben?"

Ben studied Case, and gradually began to smile. "You didn't know he trailed after you, I see. Ruben's like that. I know him pretty well. He trailed along and watched the whole thing. That's

78

what made him late getting breakfast served up."

Case squirmed. "I suppose," he said dourly, "the old devil gave it to the whole camp, blow-by-blow."

Albright's faint smile remained as he nodded, and echoed Case's words. "Blow-by-blow. Ruben's got a great imagination and he doesn't ever forget anything he wants to remember. He has his faults, and they're many, but he's loyal and he's as good a camp cook as ever lived. Another thing, Case . . . he likes you."

They stood for a time looking at one another. Then Ben, hearing a high, hooting cry down below, turned and watched Will Johns and Ferdinand Haight and Owen Wallace begin the day's drive. He smoked his cigar, viewing this dusty, colorful scene, and said over his shoulder: "What of my niece, if you draw your time and ride on?" He turned and waited for his answer to that.

Case, also seeing that great sea of dull red backs and tossing horns begin its northward ambling, said: "That'd be up to her, I reckon. Maybe if I rode on, it'd be best for her, anyway."

"Maybe," agreed Ben. "But it seems to me that should be up to her." He drew his horse in close, stepped up, and sat there, turning the cigar around in his fingers. "It takes a pretty good man, sometimes, to sweat out a bad hand when he's dealt one. Any man can just up and ride away."

He turned his horse, kneed it down off that little knoll, and when he got down to the flat again, he reined up, flicked ash from his cheroot, and sat there listening to Case Hyle's animal coming down behind him.

When the younger man drew up, Ben turned and said from a perfectly impassive face: "Take the drag like you've been doing. And just one word of advice . . . let Bass come to you. Don't you go to him."

Case rode off southwesterly in a loose lope. Ben sat a moment watching him go, then he turned, still with that grave and impassive expression, and booted out his own animal toward the point position far ahead where Bass Templeton was slouching along as the prairie sun got higher and hotter.

But Ben Albright did not go up where Bass was. He was an experienced commander of men, so he rode back a quarter of a mile, coming in behind his niece.

When she threw him her troubled and solemn look, he merely nodded, and said—"It's going to be hot again today."—and kept on riding, giving her no chance to draw him into this thing that was patently riding her spirit hard.

They kept within sight of the Trinchera this day, and did not attempt to make good time. Owen Wallace and young Will Johns cursed and stormed their way through that thorny undergrowth, chousing thirsty critters forward.

It was another idiosyncrasy of longhorns that, given the least encouragement, they will hide in shadowy bracken. Owen and Will used plaited drover's whips to pop them out of these places, while all the time their tempers got increasingly shorter and shorter.

Ruben, jolting along in the dusty wake of the drive, instead of being his usual disagreeable self, sat up there tooling his team along and singing "Lorena" at the top of his off-key, crackly old voice. He hadn't seen such a splendid battle of Titans since the war—and for this he was grateful to Case and Bass. The fight had reaffirmed his faith in this younger generation that men could still fight so fiercely and competently. He was not even worrying about that single sack of flour remaining, which must now do until they got to the border, and which would fall far short of being adequate to this.

They made a noon halt where the Trinchera's banks were smoothly clear of undergrowth for a full mile northward, the result of a bank that was as flat as the land on both sides and over which flash floods during the spring had repeatedly uprooted and washed away every growing thing excepting that wiry, hardy, and perennial forage grass.

Here, Owen and young Will complained about

the rips in their clothing and ate in a silence that was near to sullenness. Here, too, Bass Templeton stood beside his mount eating with his head down, and Case Hyle, farther back, ate the same way.

Atlanta and her uncle sat together in the shade created by their saddle horses. Twice, the beautiful girl looked up from anguished eyes, and quickly looked down again.

Only Ruben seemed entirely normal as he worked. When this meal was finished, everyone was relieved to get away from the wagon, where that tense and uncomfortable awkwardness was thick enough to cut with a knife.

Atlanta, lingering at the stirrup, was softly spoken to by Ben.

"Ride with me," he said. "Don't push things. Let time do what words never can do, girl. Come on."

They rode off together.

Bass Templeton rode straight out to point position again and Case Hyle spent a little time helping Ruben clean up, letting the herd go on past until the drag came on. Then he too got astride and joined the drive.

They were now close to twenty miles north of Lansing's Ferry, and because this other vital thing was in their minds, none of them had a single thought about those settlers and their creek-side town.

Once though, Ruben was twisting to expectorate over the wagon side, and thought he saw horsemen far back. This surprised him, so he strained to see through the heavy dust. But those riders, if indeed they were riders at all, faded out where the Trinchera made a quick bend, jutting tangled creek growth between Ruben and what he'd thought he'd seen.

He looked at the Albright riders who were farther out. They were all slouching along with the hot sunlight beating over them, unmindful of anything to their rear. He looked back again, when the drive was far enough along for those riders to come out across that clearing where they had nooned. They did not appear and Ruben gave it up. Sometimes the heat did that to a man. He recalled he'd seen Yank cavalry during the war when it'd been only bone tiredness and his imagination.

He forgot this little interlude and looped the lines at his brake handle, tilted his hat forward to shade his eyes, and tried to doze, but a stray thought came. Mr. Ben had been so absorbed by the fight between Hyle and Bass Templeton he'd forgotten to raise hell about Ruben being late with breakfast. He faintly, slyly smiled over this. Then, off on his right by the creek, came a blistering roar of profane anger. Ruben opened one eye.

Owen Wallace was coming out of a particularly

bad brush tangle, riding bent far over and holding his hat in one hand. As Ruben watched, Owen halted, shook leaves and twigs loose, crushed his hat on his head, and turned just as three steers burst clear with Will Johns popping them every jump with his whip.

The day wore along as many other days just like it had worn along—hot and humid and discomfortingly sticky. It was full of the rank smell of animal sweat, and every now and then the silence was broken by the protesting bawls of the cattle.

Stationed at the point, Bass kept pushing his steady way north. Down the herd's right side rode Ben. On the far left, a mile farther out, rode Atlanta. In the drag, hard to see because of lazy dust, came Case, his job taking more and more work as the heat grew greater, leg weariness began to bother the animals, and just plain sulky laziness caused some critters to hang back.

Ruben's team knew precisely the correct distance to observe, keeping far enough back from the critters so as not to cause them any uneasiness. They plodded along, white foam working up suds-like under collars, along flanks where traces rubbed, and around their britchings, while again Ruben tried to take a nap.

It was, in every respect, a typical hot day on the trail up out of Texas across the Staked Plains to the hungry north and its booming Kansas markets.

Finally, where clearer creekbank appeared, Owen and Will had a respite. They rode along, some two hundred feet apart, with rawhide whips coiled in hand, watching the nearest cattle leave the water for the onward press of the main drive.

This cleared bankside was not very long, though. Where willows, cottonwoods, and plum thickets grew, they began closing the distance that lay between them and the herd, closing in so that they would be in position to turn back the breakaways again. For a while none of the steers tried to get into the thicket, though.

Owen loped on and was slightly in the lead of young Will, determined to prevent a rush for the shade before it started, when a sharp sound came that wrenched Ruben upright upon his wagon seat, gasping and choking for air. He'd heard that unmistakable sound many, many times. It had never ceased to cause a frantic pounding of his heart. Now, he ducked first one way then another way, craning for the source of that flat, ripping sound. He saw nothing on either side of the wagon or behind it, either, so he sprang back into forward position and strained ahead.

Then he saw, not the source of that single, slamming rifle shot, but the effect of it.

Will Johns's horse was standing riderless, looking askance at something in the grass. Owen

Wallace was also sitting perfectly still up ahead, looking blankly back where young Will lay. As Ruben watched, Owen turned his horse and walked it back, stopped, swung down, and stood there staring. He seemed dumbfounded. Then Owen let off a keening shout, drew his hand gun, and fired it twice into the air.

Ruben fumbled at releasing the lines, taking them off the brake handle and flipping them, urging his startled team into a bolting rush over to Johns. He saw Case Hyle leave the drag on a dead run, flash past, and slide down to a halt where Owen stood, still looking stunned. Farther out, Ben had reined around. He now sat stiffly erect, looking back down the land toward Ruben's plunging wagon, and ahead of it, where Hyle and Wallace stood beside their animals. Ben was too far out to have heard anything, too close to the bellowing herd. But now he wheeled about and came loping back, obviously drawn by the stiff stance of those two riders beside Will Johns's empty saddle. He yelled to Ferdinand to stay with the herd.

Atlanta and Bass Templeton, neither having looked back, kept on riding with the herd, unaware that anything untoward had happened at all.

CHAPTER EIGHT

By the time Ruben got there, set the brake of the wagon, clambered down, and ran across the little distance to where Case and Owen stood, Ben Albright had also arrived. He strode up with long steps and halted.

There in the trampled grass lay Will Johns. No one had to kneel and roll him over to know that he was dead. A purplish round hole in the side of his head proved death to have been instantaneous.

"How did it happen?" Ben demanded of Owen Wallace.

"I don't know," answered the dark cowboy, still looking bewildered. "He was behind me. I'd just ridden ahead to chouse back some critters. I heard the shot and looked back. I figured Will had fired it, maybe to break up a run for the water by part of the herd." Owen looked down gravely. "But . . . there he is . . . dead."

Ben kept staring at Wallace. "Let me see your gun," he ordered.

Wallace's head flung up. They were all looking at him. He stood like stone, making no immediate move to comply.

Then Case said: "I think he's telling the truth, Ben. Look at that wound. Will was shot from behind. I saw Owen go loping on ahead. He couldn't have shot Will from behind."

Now Ruben spoke up, saying in his quick, nasal way: "Mister Ben, I seen Owen lope ahead, too. And I heard that shot. It come from south of my wagon, down along the creek somewheres." Ruben then had another thought. "Anyway . . . when Owen came back and saw Will lyin' here, he took out his pistol and give the distress signal. He fired twice in the air and yelled. I saw that with my own two eyes."

Albright knelt at Johns's side, thumbed back his hat, and looked a long time at the angle of that killing shot. He then pushed himself upright and looked far back along the creek.

Ruben watched this and spoke up again. "Mister Ben, half hour or so ago I thought I saw horsemen trailin' us. They appeared to be stayin' in the plum thickets, though, and I wasn't sure."

Case Hyle swung back across his animal, reining away. He said to Ben: "You'd better come with me."

Albright nodded and turned from the body. "Ruben," he ordered, "make camp! Owen, go fetch Bass and my niece. Let the herd drift to feed."

Riding together, Case and Ben Albright went south, side-by-side. Neither of them spoke until, near the creek, both dismounted to tie their horses and scout ahead afoot.

Then Ben said: "I don't understand it. Why young Will? Surely he had no enemies up here, and I don't believe he had any enemies anywhere who'd hate him enough to trail us this far."

Case had a suspicion but he kept this to himself. "I'll go down through the thicket to the creek, then angle back and forth," he said. "You take the west side."

They went carefully along in this manner, Case covering the most ground. Down here there was absolute silence, although lowing cattle could be heard in the distance and now and then a scolding brush linnet flew away as they skulked along.

"Ben!" Case called after a while. "Come down to the creekbank where I am. Over here!"

Albright came, pushing tangled creepers and weeping willow growth aside as he advanced. Case was standing in dripping shade almost entirely hidden from view when Ben got down there. Case stepped forth and pointed down at the spongy earth. He said nothing. There was nothing to say. By their tracks, four men had crossed the Trinchera here. None of their horses were shod. All the hoofs were large and had sunk deep in to the spongy soil.

Albright examined the prints a while, threw his glance on across to the Trinchera's far side, and finally looked calmly around at Case, saying: "I'm getting an idea. What do you make of it?"

"The same thing you do. The same thing I

thought when we were riding down here. But what's got me stumped, Ben, is why?"

"Yeah . . . why?"

"Not just because we tried to buy flour from them. Surely not because we wanted to pay them to ferry the chuck wagon across. It'd have to be a better reason than those."

Case turned, studying the land to the south. He plucked at a leaf and idly chewed it. There were no horsemen in sight anywhere. The land lay, as always, under its late springtime dancing heat, empty, hushed, and seemingly endless.

"They had quite a ride," said Ben. "Men wouldn't ride over twenty miles and shoot another man without a very good reason."

"Maybe that kid that Will whipped died."

But Albright shook his head. "Who dies from a couple of punches?" he said. "They wouldn't kill Will just because he fought that fellow, would they?"

Case raised his shoulders and let them fall. "How do you determine how men will react? It doesn't seem likely though. It wasn't much of a fight."

Ben stepped back into the shade and stood looking down at those tracks made by the horses of the rough settlers.

"From behind," he said after several minutes of thinking and studying the area. "Whatever their reason, a man doesn't shoot from behind."

"No."

They stood on for a while longer, both thinking, neither speaking, that creek-side humidity building up around them and the whispering rush of water making its sad, sad sound.

"Let's go back," said Ben. "We have to bury Will."

"And . . . ?"

Ben looked around, his expression stern, his pale eyes like creek bottom pebbles. "I want to know the why of this. You and Bass and I will ride to Lansing's Ferry."

Case spat out the leaf and went back through the undergrowth to his horse without saying anything. They were astride, bound for the distant wagon, when he said: "Ben, send someone for the soldiers at Fort Alert."

Albright kept on riding. He made no reply to this until they were back with the others. Then, handing his horse into Ruben Adams's care, he said to Wallace: "Owen, I want you to ride for Fort Alert. You know where it's located?"

"Yes. From here it's at least forty miles northeast," responded the swarthy cowboy.

"Take a fresh horse and go right now. Fetch back someone to look into this. You'd better say we need a cavalry company."

Wallace didn't move. He had his hard, black eyes fixed upon Ben. "You find something at the creek?" he asked.

The attention of the others came alert, awaiting Ben's answer to this. They had wrapped Will's body in an old blanket and rolled it under the wagon out of the spoiling, fiercely hot sun rays.

Ben saw Will's body there and continued to gaze at it as he said: "Yes, we found some horse tracks where four men crossed the Trinchera heading back south. Unshod, big-footed plow horses."

"Ahhh," said Bass Templeton. "Settlers. Those men from Lansing's Ferry. But why, Ben? Not over that little two-bit flurry between Will and that tomfool young settler who tried to run off a lousy four head."

"Who knows why?" Case said, and started along to turn loose his horse.

Atlanta turned a little to watch him pace along. Ruben, too, was concerned more with Case than with any of the others.

With his back to them, Ben said: "Make a grave."

Owen Wallace went to the remuda where Case was off-saddling. He looked swollen with anger. "Hyle, while I'm gone, pick off one of those settlers for me, will you?" He said more under his breath, his voice pulsing with the peculiar kind of blind and unreasoning hatred he was capable of. He snaked out a fresh animal, saddled it, and flung across its back. "I don't like to leave," he said, addressing Case. "I know what Ben's got in mind. I saw it in his face. I'd like to stick around and be in on that."

"On what?" queried Case, stepping away from his grounded gear, gazing at the dark, flat face above him.

"Ben Albright . . . he's his own kind of law," Wallace answered. "He's not going to wait for no Yank soldiers." Then he reined around and went spurring away toward the creek.

As Case watched, Wallace came to the water and did not even slow, but hooked his horse hard, making it leap far out and land with a tremendous splash. Case thought he would not like to be a horse Owen Wallace was riding when Wallace was upset or in a hurry.

Case returned to the wagon where the others were, and joined Templeton and Ruben in digging a narrow, long hole close to the willows where afternoon shade somewhat ameliorated the intense heat that made this undertaking doubly bitter.

Bass Templeton did not look even once at Case until the grave was finished. Then he shot a quick look around to say: "So those tracks were made by unshod horses?"

"Yes, unshod," Case confirmed, and then moved along to the creek as Templeton walked away. Case got down upon his knees, removed his shirt, scooped up water, and began to wash his upper torso. He heard no one approaching through his own noise, but when he stood up to let the sun dry him, Atlanta was standing back a short distance watching him. They exchanged a long look.

"My uncle wants you to saddle up," she said very soberly. "Case . . . ?"

"Yes'm?"

"If you go back there . . . it isn't going to help Will at all."

He took up his shirt, donned it, and began to button up slowly. "Your uncle wants to know why he was shot like that. So do I." He finished with the shirt, walked over to her, and stopped, looking down into her eyes. "I reckon you want to know about the fight," he said. "Well, it was about as everyone thinks. Atlanta, tell me something. Did Bass have a right to feel as he felt about you?"

"If you mean, did I encourage him. The answer is no. He was helpful and he was friendly. There was nothing more in my mind." She started past. He detained her with a quick, outflung hand. "One more question . . . have you regrets about that kiss?"

She looked at him for a long time before answering. He was tall and broad-shouldered, and, like most range men, he was slim of hip and loose moving. He wasn't a polished man. He wasn't flamboyant or spectacular. He was quiet and, she knew from the burn of his lips, he was powerfully motivated.

These thoughts came to her now and couldn't be brushed from her mind. He was a person, like her uncle, who she watched with an interest that never diminished. He had a way of reassuring her simply by standing close, of binding her to him with his quietness and his strength. Behind his silence, his easy-going patience, there was something about him that never failed to lift her heart. She had thought about what he'd told her that other time—about men facing ostracism for the things they believed in—and she thought he was wholly right about what he'd done, even though being in agreement with him made her feel, in some way, as though she were a traitor to her own kind.

Finally, she said: "No, Case, I don't regret that kiss." Then she left him standing there, retracing her way back toward Ruben's wagon.

By the time Case got back, Ben and the others had placed young Will in his grave. They were covering him now. When they were finished, Ben got his Bible from the wagon and read from it.

Off in the hazy west that afternoon a reddish glow was firming up, was winnowing heat from baked earth, and softening full daylight's yellow harshness.

Having come in from the herd, Ferdinand

joined the others. They now stood, bareheaded, as Ben finished, closed his Bible, and then stood there looking far out on to the plains in a manner that made it appear that he could hear distant voices.

Ruben sniffled, ran a limp shirt sleeve along his upper lip, then stepped away, heading to his chuck wagon. There, he grunted up over the tailgate, was gone from sight for a bit before reappearing. He had a little fire going, so he poured out five cups of black coffee and then waited for the others to come along.

Bass Templeton walked with Ben as far as the wagon. Case and Atlanta strolled silently behind them. There were peculiar currents in the camp atmosphere now—roiled and confusing and overlapping.

Ben put away his Bible and took a cup from Ruben. He leaned in the reddening shade at the side of the wagon to sip his coffee. Eventually, he said very quietly, without looking at either man: "Bass, you and Case go saddle up. We got a long ride ahead of us. Ferd, get back out to the herd after you eat something."

Case saw Atlanta gazing steadily at him. He hesitated, returned that look for a moment, then moved out, trailing Templeton, toward the rope corral Ruben had thrown up to hold their saddle stock.

Atlanta glided over to her uncle's side. She

said: "Please be careful, Uncle Ben. Please don't make it any worse."

He emptied the cup and tossed it into one of Ruben's water buckets. His saddled horse was tied close at hand. "How," he asked the beautiful girl, "do you make a murder worse?"

"By another murder," she murmured to him.

He bent to untie his reins. "Not murder, Atlanta," he said. "I never was a part to anything like murder in my life. I hold that to be the worst crime a man can commit." He faced her, holding the reins. "Whoever fired that shot was a murderer. Young Will had no chance at all. That man is a murderer and I want to see him pay for that. It's got to be like that, girl . . . else every coward in Texas can shoot his enemies from behind."

Ben mounted up. He looked along where Ruben was banking his fire. In a louder voice, he called forward: "Ruben, you keep a sharp eye, you hear? You'll be responsible for Atlanta till we get back."

Ruben sprang up, wiped his palms upon his legs, and bobbed his head up and down. "Yes, sir, Mister Ben," he replied. "Yes, sir. I'll keep a sharp watch."

Bass Templeton and Case Hyle rode over to Ben. Case looked down into Atlanta's face, but Bass, his expression grim and toughly set, kept his stare fully ahead upon Ben.

"Ready?" Templeton said.

Ben nodded, and the three of them wheeled, loping southward through that thickening red glow.

CHAPTER NINE

Tough Texas horses can cover a lot of ground when they have to. Ben Albright and Bass Templeton and Case Hyle crossed the Trinchera where the four Lansing's Ferry riders had crossed earlier.

It was here that Bass made a good observation. "Even if we rode unshod horses, too," he said, "it still couldn't have been any of us. None of our crew has crossed the creek since Lansing's Ferry."

They rode along, following the southbound tracks as long as daylight permitted. They had covered a goodly distance by then. Dusk did not come to the Staked Plains in summertime until early night was upon the land.

When it was no longer possible to see the tracks, they held steadily to the same course those other riders had held to, and halted only once to smoke a cigarette, rest their animals, and stand in gloomy silence, each thinking their own private thoughts.

Then they pushed onward again, and on the sundown side of midnight came across their first soddie with its slab-sided noisy dogs, its miserly little orange lamp glow, and its squalid wretchedness.

Templeton wrinkled his nose. "Pigs," he said distastefully, and halted when Ben drew down to gaze ahead, orienting their position in his mind.

"Never could understand why people would pen-up pigs."

The settler's barking dogs were in a frenzy now. They did not, however, make any rush out upon the plain where the three Texans quietly sat their saddles.

"A little east of here," murmured Case. "Then south."

Ben nodded, lifted his rein hand, and led them along in a gallop far out and around the homestead, bearing in the direction Case had mentioned.

It was after midnight when they approached Lansing's Ferry from the north, riding slowly down upon it with a scimitar moon over their shoulders and the diamond-like glitter of countless stars putting a gentle, soft light over everything.

"I want to see their marshal or sheriff or whatever they call him," said Ben, steadying his horse into a dusty pair of wagon ruts, which marked a north-south roadway into the village. "We're not here for trouble . . . yet. So, let's be careful."

There were very few lights in Lansing's Ferry as the three of them came swinging along, passing through the environs, and slowly pacing their way down over the main roadway. A few dogs barked, sensing the strangeness of these riders in the quiet night, but otherwise they went unheeded.

"There," Case announced suddenly, pointing with his free right hand. "Where those carriage lamps are mounted on either side of the door. That sign says 'Town Marshal.' "

Ben reined toward a badly cribbed hitch rack and got down. He stood, while waiting for Case and Templeton to come alongside, and looked up and down Lansing's Ferry's central thoroughfare.

"It's changed a lot since last summer," he said idly to his riders. "Old Lansing wouldn't recognize it now."

"Smells different, too," mumbled Bass, and, having dismounted, stumped up onto the boardwalk to look at the town marshal's office. "This used to be old Lansing's storage shed, didn't it, Ben?"

Albright nodded, passed up to the door, opened it, and blinked at the quick rush of orange light that rushed over the three of them.

A thickly made, slovenly looking man was sound asleep in a tilted-back desk chair, his low-heeled settler boots delicately balanced upon a littered, scarred old roll-top desk.

Ben went up to this man, considered the dull badge upon his vest, and put forth a gloved hand.

"Come alive, mister," he said, gently shaking the town marshal. "Come alive, there."

The burly man opened both his eyes without moving any other part of his body. He looked impassively at all three Texans, then slowly took down his feet, squared around in the chair, and yawned mightily. "What's on your mind?" he said to Ben, then flung up his head quickly, putting a wide stare forward.

Case watched the cobwebs leave the man's mind in a flash. The lawman had recognized Albright in that second and was suddenly and awkwardly alert and wary. He sat there looking quickly from one face to the next, before his expression changed, becoming hard and unpleasant and tough.

"You got a lot of nerve coming here," he told Ben.

Albright continued to regard the lawman for a moment before saying to him: "Mister, a settler shot and killed one of my riders this afternoon. Slipped up on us in the brush along the Trinchera and shot my rider in the head . . . from behind."

The town marshal listened to this with his look still wary. Then he began to scowl. "I don't believe that," he grumbled as he got to his feet. He was shorter than any of the three Texans but he was broader than any of them. "A settler you say. How do you know that . . . did you see him?"

"If we'd seen him," responded Bass Templeton in a growl, "we wouldn't be here now. And he wouldn't have ridden off afterward, either."

The marshal looked at Bass. "Then how do you know it was a settler?" he demanded.

"We found the tracks of this man and his three companions," answered Ben. "We trailed them. That's how we know."

"No," muttered the lawman, "you gotta have better evidence than that."

"And one of my men saw them from a distance. They looked to him like men from Lansing's Ferry."

The marshal gradually assumed a troubled look. He said: "Mister Albright, this town is het up against Texas herds and herders. There's been bad trouble, and your man whipping Charley Connelly's boy, Patrick, the other day didn't help none. But I can't imagine anyone here trailin' you, and then bushwhackin' one of your cowboys. Hell, if folks felt like that, they'd have bushwhacked some of Higgins's crew, or some of Colonel Bee's riders, last year. Those two trail bosses did a heap more to cause bad blood than you've done."

"That," said Case Hyle, speaking for the first time, "is exactly what's got us puzzled. Marshal, the man who shot Will Johns was a settler. We're satisfied about this. What we want to know is why he shot him?"

"From behind," Templeton added coldly. "The way a coward shoots a man."

The village law officer looked at Ben, then at Bass, and finally at Case Hyle. "You're sure it wasn't one of your own men?" he said. "You're plumb sure of that?"

"Plumb sure," stated Ben Albright. "And we're sure he was shot and that he's dead."

The lawman twisted around, felt behind for his desk, eased up onto it, and perched there, swinging one thick leg. "Who would've done it?" he asked.

"You say that lad our man whipped was Connelly's son?"

"He was."

"Well, Marshal," Ben said coldly, "that man we lost was the same lad who whipped Connelly's boy. Does that bring anything to mind for you?"

The marshal looked incredulous. He squinted over at Ben. "Are you sayin' Charley did this?"

"I'm saying he might have thought he had a reason for doing it, but I don't know who actually shot my rider. I only aim to find out who that murderer was and why he did it."

"I see. And when you find out . . . what then, Mister Albright?"

Ben began drawing on his gloves. He concentrated upon this chore while he answered, saying: "Marshal, I believe in the law. Maybe not your kind of law, but in legal justice. All I'll tell you now is that whoever shot my rider is going to pay for it . . . to the hilt."

Ben put a cold glance upon the marshal, watching his face. Off to one side, Bass Templeton and Case Hyle stood in solid silence.

The marshal stopped swinging his leg and ran a hand over his face, then put a brittle glare upon Ben.

"You hear what happened to Colonel Bee last year?" he asked. "Well, don't you go and make the same mistake he did, Mister Albright. There are too many here in Lansing's Ferry for you people to ride roughshod over. They mostly got their bitter memories, too. The war hasn't been over so long we've forgotten which side Texas was on."

Albright heard the lawman out, then in a soft tone he said: "Marshal, I've been wondering if that mightn't have been behind that murder. If I was sure of that . . ." Ben checked himself. He stood there looking from uncompromising eyes, before he continued: "If anyone is making a mistake, you are. There are six Texans with my drive. They are equal to fifty of your sodbusters. If they want to renew the war, why I reckon Lansing's Ferry is as good a place as any other to do it." Ben was moving toward the door now, his eyes iron-like.

The marshal slipped down from his perch on the desk. "Wait!" he called swiftly. "Just

105

a minute, Mister Albright. You couldn't win, but that's not what's in my mind right now. I don't hold with murder . . . not even of a Rebel. Tell me something . . . how far north did this happen?"

"Twenty, twenty-five miles."

"And you said there were four men involved?"

"Yes."

"And you tracked them here?"

"No," corrected Ben. "I didn't say that. I said we tracked them, determined they rode big, unshod settler horses. They came south in this direction, but when it got dark we couldn't follow them any farther."

The marshal was silent for several moments. He paced once across his little office and back again. Wearing a full scowl as he came to a halt, he said: "Mister Albright, I want you to go on back to your camp. Don't stay the night here in Lansing's Ferry. It'd get folks all fired-up again. You go on back and lie over tomorrow. I'll hunt you up after I've done a little nosin' around." He stopped, turned, and gazed steadily at Ben. "Will you do that for me?"

Ben Albright nodded. "We're camped west of the creek. You can't miss us. The herd is scattered out over a considerable distance. We'll be waiting, Marshal," Ben said, and reached for the door latch. "One more thing, Marshal. I'll have men posted as sentinels. When you come up,

106

make some noise. I don't propose to be caught off guard again in case someone other than you comes slipping up with murder in mind."

Ben passed out of the office. Bass Templeton was right behind him. Case Hyle, just before leaving, said: "Marshal, what's your name?"

"Conrad Beal, cowboy. What's yours?"

"Case Hyle."

"And that other big feller?"

"Bass Templeton. He's Mister Albright's herd boss."

Marshal Beal nodded. "Don't let them stop for the night anywhere around here," he warned. "I'll see you fellows again."

Outside the office, Case was the last man to mount up. On either side of him Bass Templeton and Ben Albright sat waiting, studying the town carefully.

The three of them eased around and rode north out of Lansing's Ferry. Beyond town a mile, Bass said: "I could use some strong black coffee." Neither of his companions said anything to this. Bass slumped in his saddle, silent and looking frustrated.

They cut west to the creek and followed it for several hours. As they neared a wide, scarcely moving pool silvered by the moon, Ben slowed and swung down to water his animal. When his companions were on the ground, he lit a cigar and said: "I got the impression that sodbuster marshal had something on his mind after we'd talked for a spell."

"Me, too," echoed Bass. "I also got the impression he didn't like what he was thinking."

Case made a smoke. He listened to the horses sucking aerated water around the crickets of their spade bits for several seconds before saying: "He seemed like a fair man. Not particularly friendly toward Texans, but fair," he observed. "I guess, being like he is, we couldn't expect him to feel different."

Bass Templeton regarded Case steadily. It was the first time he'd done this since their fight. He appeared to be agreeing with what Case had just said. Then he turned away, led his horse north a little, trailed out to the length of the reins, and got down belly-flat to drink. He was upstream from the other two men. Ben and Case also tanked up after their mounts were full.

After mounting, the three of them splashed over to the west bank and turned north again, riding through a night full of shifting creek-side shadows and deep silence.

It was some time before they heard the faint lowing of cattle, intermittent and drowsy sounding. They sighted the first critters shortly before they saw Ruben's little fire burning steadily and set their course by this beacon.

As they came onto the main herd, Ben declared: "Owen should be at Fort Alert by this time. With luck, he'll be back tomorrow morning with a patrol."

"Maybe we won't need Yank soldiers," said Bass.

Case shook his head at this. "It's peaceful now, but I've got a feeling about this thing," he commented. "A man doesn't kill like that unknown settler did, then just forget it. He had three others with him. The four of them were all cocked and primed. I think we'll need those soldiers all right."

Bass heard Case out, then exclaimed in a thin, antagonistic way: "If they come again, I hope it's before the Yankees get here! That way maybe we can get in our licks. After the soldiers arrive . . . no chance for evening up the score for Will."

Albright rode along, listening but saying nothing. When they were close enough to make out Ruben's wagon, he sang out an identifying call, got back a mightily relieved cry from Ruben, who had heard riders approaching and who had snatched up his saddle gun and taken a position under the chuck wagon. Then, when they rode in, Ruben came scrabbling out from under the wagon, wearing a broad and satisfied grin.

CHAPTER TEN

Ruben had his big graniteware coffee pot sitting on the stones at the edge of the fire. He hopped around, filling four cups, and when the three returning men came forth from the direction of the rope corral, Ruben's long, thin mouth cut a quick grin across his cheeks. He laughed in a way that plainly said he hadn't felt easy being all alone at the campsite with Atlanta, and that softly lighted distant grave, through the watch hours of this warm night.

"I'll fetch you some dry pants," he said to Ben. "Here, drink up . . . the coffee's good and hot."

"Never mind the pants," responded Ben, dropping down and reaching out for the cup. "I'm near dry, anyway." He took a swallow of the coffee and leaned his shoulders against a wagon wheel, looking around. "Been quiet like this all night?" he asked.

"Quiet as a church, Mister Ben. Quiet enough to hear a Comanche step on a twig a quarter mile out."

"I wasn't thinking of Comanches," muttered Ben right before he yawned.

"No problem with the herd, either, Mister Ben," Ruben advised his boss. "Ferd came in a little while ago. You didn't have no trouble in town?"

"No trouble, Ruben. Their town marshal, Conrad Beal, will be out here tomorrow afternoon or evening. So, for now, we're to lay over for a day, maybe two."

"Sure, Mister Ben. The critters need a little rest anyway."

Bass Templeton, swishing his coffee and gazing down into it, said: "Ruben, it sure would help if we had a little dram of spirits in this black coffee." He looked up at the drive's cook.

Ruben, over behind Ben, scratched his ribs and made a shocked scowl after glancing at his boss. "Not on a drive," he said. "You know Mister Ben's orders. No whiskey drinkin' on the trail."

Bass looked down into his cup again. He glumly nodded at this admonition. Then he shot another look over at the cook. His gaze was sly. "No law against a man taking precautions against snakebite though, is there?"

Smiling, Ben got up, put aside his cup, and without a word went around the wagon to his bedroll. They heard him drop down there, grunt his boots off, and lay back. He let off a long, loud sigh.

Case Hyle refilled his cup and sat down again, legs crossed under him, face thoughtful, and his thick shoulders hunched forward.

Ruben gazed for a while upon the two big men sitting in deep silence, before he scrambled under his wagon, scuffed a moment or two in the dust, and emerged to spring upright with a bottle in one hand and the forefinger of his other hand held over his lips. He moved forward and carefully measured out a trickling of this precious whiskey into both of their cups. Then he slipped back under the wagon to restore the bottle to its hiding place.

The three of them sat on, sipping and saying nothing.

Ruben poked at his little fire that was slowly dying. His proddings only produced a little sifting of sparks. Finally, he said: "Sure miss young Will. You know, one time he told me about artillery fire durin' the war levelin' their home and killin' his folks."

"Damned Yankees," growled Templeton.

"No," said Ruben quickly. "No, it was *our* cannon, Bass. He told me the barrels were plumb shot smooth and the shells fell a half mile short . . . smack dab on his folks' place."

Bass drank and swished the liquid in his cup and didn't speak again for a long time. He seemed to have suddenly become very aware that he was sitting beside Case Hyle. He drained his cup, put it down, turned, and got up. "It's been a long night," he muttered, and went off toward his bedroll.

Ruben put his bright, raffish stare upon Case. "See," he said. "Bass don't carry no grudges."

Case let this pass. He said: "How was Miss Atlanta after we rode away?"

"All right I reckon. She got into the wagon and didn't come back out. I made her coffee, but she didn't want it."

Case turned this over in his mind and stood up. "Thanks for the coffee," he said to Ruben, then stood up and moved over to his blankets.

Fully clothed, he lay back to consider the heavens and wonder in his mind if Atlanta's refusal of Ruben's coffee did not have something to do with the fear he felt was in her. He thought of other things, his mind drifting aimlessly as a tired man's mind often does, and had no idea when sleep came, or how long he'd been asleep, when the dull, throaty smash of a six-gun shot brought him back to full consciousness with a pounding heart. He reached for his own pistol, rolled off the blankets, and sat up. Another shot came, then a flurry of them, and after that high, whooping yells in the pit of the westerly night.

Over by the wagon Ruben Adams let off a bawl of frightened alarm. He was a dimly visible blur, moving jerkily against the bronze glow of the firelight coals.

West of Case, the lanky frame of Bass Templeton came whirling up off the ground to stand a second in crouched bewilderment, then sink as swiftly down to earth again.

Case struggled to clear sleep's deep dregs from his senses and locate those gunshots. They were off in the west, but they were shifting, moving, never twice erupting in the same place.

Ben Albright's roaring shout crashed over those other sounds. "Stampede!" he cried. "It's a stampede!"

Case felt the earth begin to quiver out where he lay. The air seemed to reverberate, making it impossible right then to determine the direction those panicked animals were running. Shock waves filled the roundabout night and that chilling thunder of two thousand animals with their wickedly sharp horns blindly running was increasing steadily.

Case sprang up and ran on to the wagon, calling out for Atlanta, a knot in his stomach. Then she was there, hastily dressed, her thick hair cascading darkly over her shoulders. Her face in the light of the moon appeared white with terror and her eyes stood out as black as the pit of the night.

Bass Templeton came up at the same instant Ben rushed around to the others. Case said loudly: "From the west. Someone is stampeding them toward us . . . over us!" He did not wait for Ben's orders. He caught Atlanta roughly by one arm and wheeled away, running on for the creek-side thicket, and beyond it to the waterway itself. Back a short distance, came Ruben, his crippled gait impeding him only slightly. Farther back Ben and Bass were running.

Those gun shots were closer now. The high-pitched yells of excited riders rose up through the crash of thunder. Case battered his way straight through the underbrush to the water's edge, still tightly holding onto Atlanta. Arriving at the bank, he said quickly: "Keep hold of my hand. I know you can't swim, but this is the only way. No matter what, don't break away from me. Now let's go."

They went down into the current, Case bracing his legs sturdily against its suck and pull. Atlanta stepped over to him, her hand locked with surprising strength to his.

Crashing their way to the water behind Ruben, Ben Albright and Bass Templeton fought through the undergrowth, came suddenly out upon the bank, hesitated only a second, then lunged ahead into water up to their hips. Ruben had paused upon the bank, gasping, before he finally walked in. Consequently, he was the last man in. He had both arms outstretched as far as possible, clinging to a spindly willow that bent ominously and moaned at his desperate hold. As the water swept Ruben's feet out from under him, the willow strained low, near to breaking, before Ruben got his footing and stood up again, shaking all over.

Case squatted low to peer out beneath the underbrush along the creekbank. In this position, he sighted gun flashes right before he saw the frenzied press of dull red bodies appear out of the darkness. As he stared, the leaders of the stampede struck the chuck wagon. He watched in disbelief as the wagon rose up, teetered a second on two wheels, then crashed over onto its side, spilling everything in it upon the ground. The sound of the splintering of the wood echoed through his head.

But then his attention was drawn to those long, wide, and graceful, but very deadly horns glistening in the moonlight as the longhorns headed toward the Trinchera. So closely packed were those rampaging steers that the constant click and rattle of those horns striking, sliding over each other, coming hard against solid objects, made a chilling sound, more frightening than even the gunshots farther back.

Case straightened up, turned, and put his lips close to Atlanta's head. "The wagon is gone!" he shouted. "They'll hit the underbrush now."

Just then Ruben let out a yell as the willow broke, and they all turned in time to see his flailing arms beat frantically upon the water's surface if only for a moment as he was swept up in the current heading south. In a twinkling, he was gone in the trembling darkness.

Simultaneously with Ruben's disappearance the first wild steers, forced ahead by the animals behind them, struck into the thicket, tearing up willows and snapping wild grape runners as though they had been twine. The first longhorns went a full fifty feet before the matted undergrowth held them hanging while other animals piled up against and over them.

Case took Atlanta ten feet farther out into the water. Here, the current thrust turgidly against him, pulling at his legs, eating at the gravelly shoal where his boots were planted down stubbornly. Atlanta still clung to his left hand as she bobbed in the water. She was panting with fear. Upon the sandy shore, dead ahead, a maddened, red-eyed appeared. They could see in the moonlight that he was leaking blood from a dozen deep gashes and that at sight of Ben, who had remained close to the creekbank with his gun cocked, he dropped his head, let off a bellow, and pawed once. Ben's gun hand flashed red. The steer stood there, staring dumbly. Then he collapsed, shot dead-center in the forehead where his hair whorl was.

Other steers were bawling deafeningly as they threshed and fought one another in the thicket. Against the high sky the stiffly topped cottonwoods shook while lesser trees swayed wildly then disappeared as they were uprooted by the solid shock of those hundreds of big bovine bodies piled up.

Case was rigid, watching for animals that might break clear and make it into the creek. He was not even conscious that the stampeders were no longer firing or trying to encourage and prolong the stampede until, off to his right, he saw a small group of run-down cattle appear upon the bank. These animals stood with heaving ribs and lolling tongues, their glistening hides oozing blood from passage through the underbrush. They stood still, though, swinging foamy muzzles left and right but making no move to go into the water.

He waited several minutes before slowly making his way back toward shallow water, one foot at a time and drawing Atlanta with him. She kept her balance until, six or eight feet farther on, one foot hooked under a buried snag. She screamed as she fell. Case braced himself, tightening his grip around her hand and wrist, preventing her from being swept away as Ruben had been. She came up close by him, gasping, coughing, frightened. A little locket lay exposed between the hardness of her breasts, torn free from beneath her blouse. It reflected the moonlight, drawing his attention downward briefly.

"Case," she panted. "Save yourself."

He pulled her steadily in. "It's shallow here. Don't let go!" he warned her. Then, when she was up against him, Case put both arms around her, holding her to him, feeling the tremor that passed the full length of her. She braced backward to see his face. Then she put up both hands, caught his face, drew it down to hers, and kissed him fiercely upon the lips. His arms tightened until her breath burst raggedly against his cheek. He met her tumultuous fire with a savagery of his own. Then they turned, his arm still supporting her, and made their way cautiously toward the bank.

With their backs to the couple farther out in the Trinchera, Bass Templeton and Ben Albright saw none of this. Ben had his handgun up, alert for any steer that might make a break and head for the water. A few did appear, then a few more, and finally the creekbank was lined north and south with panting longhorns. But the madness was out of them. The animals were spent and weary from their charge. They simply hung there, stiff-legged, to hold back the rearward pressure, looking dumbly out at the humans in the water.

It was over.

Ben twisted in time to see Case leading his niece toward shore. He started in that direction himself, still holding his gun hand high and taking careful steps. Behind him, Bass saw Atlanta off on his right with Case Hyle's arm tightly around her. He stood for a heavy long moment watching the couple make it to shallow water. Then he finally started forward.

Those steers farther back began to fight the underbrush, to turn and push against other animals farther west. Here and there a few animals broke out of the thicket and went shambling back the way they had come, tails wringing from the torment of thorn-pin gouges, slavering mouths emitting a low and hoarse bawling.

A slight dawn breeze stirred a ripped piece of the chuck wagon's canvas, making it ripple and flop upon the ground. The longhorns nearest this new cause for panic, dropped their heads menacingly, bawled, and went jogging away. An hour earlier this spooky sight would have sent them headlong. Now they were too run out.

Soon dawn came to illuminate the land with its washy paleness, to give substance to the air with its powerful cattle scent and its dusty heaviness. Somewhere, a long way off, a horse whistled in its distracted way, separated from the other horses and anxious about them. There was no answering neigh for a while, then, off in the dim east across the Trinchera, came a reply to this first call.

Case, just breaking clear of the creek-side tangle of smashed growth, heard those calls. He estimated where each horse was, before pausing to say to Atlanta: "We're sure afoot now."

She took his hand and squeezed it. "But we're alive, Case. I wasn't sure a while ago that we would be."

CHAPTER ELEVEN

They stood there in solemn silence, looking at Ruben's wrecked wagon, at its trampled supplies and its broken bows, tongue, and tailgate. Each of them thought of Ruben.

They were still thinking of him when Ben said: "Bass, you and Case go take your lariats and see if you can catch the horses. And keep an eye out for Ferd. Let's hope he's not hurt." Albright's bitter stare fell upon his niece. "You'd better salvage some fresh clothing," he said, his tone crisp. Then, as the others began moving, he called to Templeton: "Find your guns . . . take them, too! I don't think those stampeders will be around, but take guns, anyway." Then Ben headed toward the creek, obviously bent upon making a southerly search along the banks for Ruben Adams.

Without thinking, Case addressed Bass, saying: "He never lets down, does he?"

"No," Bass answered. "And he never forgets, either."

They went to their bedrolls, which they found shredded. Although their saddles, bridles, and guns had been trampled upon, they were not irredeemably mauled. Then they set off in a westerly direction together.

Out a mile, Templeton said: "We'll split up here. You go north. I'll keep on west."

After that, Case was alone upon the pale prairie, his only ambulatory companions the run-out steers who put baleful glances upon him but did no more than trot away.

To the north, the land broke up after a while, becoming a series of storm gashes, some deep enough to hide mounted men within. Here, Case came upon a few small bands of Albright steers that had not been involved in the stampede. But the abrupt appearance among them of a man on foot caused these creatures to bolt in a miniature stampede of their own. They were typical of their range-bred kind. They distrusted mounted men but were accustomed to seeing them. A man on foot, however, was something else again. They would run wildly at the first sight of an unmounted person.

Case had with him his Winchester carbine, his lariat, and his six-gun in its now soggy holster. There was a tiredness in him that went all the way down to his spirit. Twice, when he encountered sweet water springs, he was tempted to lie down, just for a little while, and close his eyes. He did not, however, do this, but kept on, while all around him that first light steadily firmed up toward daylight's yellow glowing, and objects close by and far out began to assume their everyday shapes.

He thought of the stampede, of the men who had caused it, and there was no distinction, in his mind, between those men and the ones who had stealthily stalked the Albright herd to shoot and kill young Will Johns.

He thought of Atlanta, too. Of the hardness of her and of that savage kiss at the creek. He knew little of women, but he did not believe that kiss had been more than a way of showing him her gratefulness for what he'd done. He wanted very much to think it meant something else, but he was a man of rare delusions. So he did not now try to read into an event what his common sense told him had never been there.

He thought, too, of Ruben and Ferd. He heard with painful, sere clarity, Ruben's cry as he'd been swept away. He doubted very much that Ben would be able to find him. Doubted very much that anyone would see Ruben Adams again. He was hopeful about Ferd, though, figuring he would have ridden in the opposite direction when the herd took off. Unless he had been shot by the men who had caused the stampede.

The sun came. It jumped over the farthest dip of prairie as it customarily did in summertime, burning the last of night's lingering haziness from the land, leaving everything clear and sharply limned and recognizable.

Case paused upon a little rise to let that first heat work its pleasant magic upon his tired, wet, and sluggish body. He turned to look back in the direction of camp. Cattle were scattered everywhere and in bunches, grazing along contentedly now as though there had never been a stampede. Then he turned north again to study the route he must take, and at once saw, deep in the brushy arroyo on his right, an Albright horse standing stocked up and quiet, beside a stunted juniper tree.

For a long while Case stood utterly still. He looked around for other horses, saw none, and concluded that this was the horse he'd heard call to the animals he'd become separated from in the wild night. He traced out a way to get down into the arroyo without making noise. His intentness sparked from some hidden inner reservoir, a fresh lift of energy.

Leaving his carbine behind upon the little hill, Case began working his way silently down with endless patience. He could not afford to miss his lariat cast at this horse. As far as he knew, it was the only Albright mount still within tracking distance.

It took him the better part of an hour to get into the arroyo without making a sound. Another quarter hour to get within fifty feet of the drowsing horse and build his loop. There would be no time for the usual steadying whirls that gave a thrown lariat its momentum. He knew that as soon as he spun that rope, the range-wise horse would identify that faintly hissing sound and bolt.

Case carefully flipped his rope to one side and slightly behind him. He had to use the wild-horse cast, which was simply to have the loop upon the ground, open and ready, then, when the moment arrived to throw, to make one high-dropping overhand cast. This type of cast was never guaranteed and it entirely lacked momentum, but it at least gave the roper one chance where otherwise he'd have none.

The horse switched his tail at flies and smacked his lips. He looked up slightly, stamped once, then again, and flung his head. That was when Case staked everything on his overhand throw. The horse, sighting movement dead ahead, flung up its head. Case's wild-horse loop fell smoothly and drew up snug. Horse and cowboy stood motionless, watching one another. Then the animal succumbed to that familiar tug, and walked up to the man who had captured him.

Case recognized this animal as a beast Bass Templeton often rode. He was large, raw-boned, and tiger-striped along his lower legs. He was what Southwesterners and Mexicans called a grulla, meaning that he was a blue horse, or the color of bluish earth. It was the color of the cranes that inhabited Texas's lowland marshes. Grulla horses were noted for rugged durability and great stamina.

Case fashioned a war bridle from his lariat's turks-head end, fitted this to the grulla's head and under his upper lip, then sprang upon his bare back. The horse proved sensible, which was not usual among cowboy-broke range horses who were never ridden bareback. He responded willingly to Case's heels and climbed up out of the arroyo.

Upon the plain again, Case retrieved his carbine and set a course for camp. He was still over a mile out when he sighted Bass Templeton riding toward their base. Bass was bareback, too. He had found two horses—riding one and leading the other. Case recognized the one that was being led as the animal Will Johns had been riding when he'd been killed. He knew, from that sighting, that it was no accident that Bass led this horse and rode the other animal.

They came together a half mile out. Bass regarded the grulla and nodded, but he did not speak. They entered camp like this, side-by-side, but silent. Atlanta was working at the cook fire. She'd knotted her hair at the back of her neck with a little green ribbon, and she had on fresh clothing. She stood up to smile as Case and Bass Templeton rode in.

"Uncle Ben isn't back yet, and I'm afraid you won't like my cooking," she said by way of relieved greeting. Then she shrugged, adding: "But I'm afraid you'll have to endure it."

Case made a lariat corral, turned their three horses into it, and went along where Bass stood close to Atlanta, looking glum and bone-weary. Atlanta smiled at Case, her eyes following him as he walked, and lingering upon him once he stopped.

Bass saw this. His only reaction was to hunch by the fire and reach for a tin cup with coffee in it.

"You two might as well stay here," he muttered. "I'll go see what's keeping Ben."

Atlanta, seeing Case put a considering gaze upon the squatting man, let her smile diminish. She felt something come between these two big men. Something she was no part of at all.

Case studied Atlanta for moment. "We'll both go," he said finally.

Bass did not look up, but he growled: "What's the sense of that? We're both plumb wore to a frazzle. One of us might as well rest up."

Case nodded and took the cup Atlanta was holding out to him without looking at her. He sipped the coffee and spoke over the cup's dented lip. "We'll both go," he reiterated firmly. He quickly drained off the coffee and handed Atlanta the cup, saying: "Which way did your uncle go?"

"Toward the south . . . along the creek." Atlanta looked first at Case, then Bass. She raised her gaze and looked up and down along the creek.

"He'll come walking out of there any minute now," she said with a confidence she did not feel. "Why don't you both rest until he returns?"

Bass rose, slapped dust from his trousers without looking at either of them, then shuffled away toward the horses.

Atlanta, watching him do this, said softly to Case: "He's angry."

"Bitter would come closer," Case opined. "In his boots . . . I'd feel the same way. He's lost you and a couple of old friends, all in a matter of a couple of days. Any sign of Ferd?"

"Nothing. Did you see any . . . ?" Atlanta began.

Shaking his head, Case started forward. He hadn't covered a hundred feet when Atlanta called to him: "Uncle Ben's coming . . . there through the thicket."

Case twisted to look back. Bass had heard Atlanta call out, and he stopped what he was doing to squint southward.

Ben Albright stepped clear of the last underbrush, halted to make a quick examination of the onward camp, then walked forward with his head up and his arms swinging. By the time he got to the wrecked wagon, Case and Bass were already waiting there as Atlanta got another cup of hot coffee.

"Well," Ben stated flatly, "he got out about a mile downstream. I found his tracks where he caught hold of a hanging willow and pulled himself up onto the sand." Ben paused to accept the cup Atlanta offered, drank, then said: "But someone got to him before I did. I tracked him clear of the brush out onto the plain. It looks as though he came upon some riders out there. . . ." Ben became quiet. After several seconds, he looked up at Bass and Case Hyle. He raised and lowered his shoulders with strong meaning.

"How many riders did he meet?" asked Case.

"Hard to say from the way the ground had been churned up, but I'd guess maybe six."

Bass scowled and scratched his side with his thumb. "Six," he muttered. "Then if it was that same four Ruben said he saw when Will was killed, they picked up reinforcements to stampede the cattle."

Again, Ben lifted and dropped his shoulders, nodding his head. He finished the coffee, put a gauging eye upon the midmorning sun, then shifted it over to the three horses that had been put in the corral. "Good work," he commented, referring to the mounts. "I guess we'd better sleep a little, then hit the trail. We'll search for Ferd at the same time."

Neither Case nor Bass asked what direction Ben proposed they ride in. They knew.

Atlanta, standing in the meager shade provided by the upturned wagon, had said nothing throughout this conversation. Her attention had been riveted to the south. Now, pointing, she spoke in a husky tone: "There are horsemen approaching from the south, Uncle Ben." She continued to look in that direction as the men shifted and turned warily.

Case moved first, after studying the riders. He ran for his carbine, and on the way scooped up Templeton's saddle gun, too. He trotted back, called out to Bass, and, when Templeton turned, threw him his weapon.

Ben stood stockstill, trying to assess those oncoming men. They rode bunched up and slow-paced. He knew they were settlers, which was obvious from their attire, their horses, as well as the way they sat their saddles. They made no attempt at concealment. In fact, they appeared to be making an issue of staying well clear of the creek-side growth so they would be seen.

Without taking his eyes off the riders, Ben instructed the others: "Atlanta, you go around on the other side of the wagon with Bass. Case, you get up front of the wagon and cover me from there. Don't shoot unless I tell you to, but keep a close watch."

Bass had to pluck at Atlanta's sleeve before her rigid fascination was broken. Then she went with him to the wagon's far side. Case Hyle stepped away, took a position amid the wagon wreckage, and knelt, resting his carbine upon the splintered brake handle before cocking the weapon. He bent low to catch those oncoming men over his sights and bring the foremost of them down the barrel to him. It was then that he saw something that made him stiffen and raise his head swiftly for a better look. One of the settlers was riding double. And the man behind his saddle looked to be Ruben Adams. Case's sharp eyes saw that Ruben seemed little the worse for his ordeal, although he looked wet and bedraggled.

Case called to Ben: "They've got Ruben."

"I know. I can see," came back in answer to this.

"That's why they're so bold. He's a hostage," Bass opined.

"No," said Ben, "I think not. Take another look at that burly man in front. I'm pretty sure that's the town marshal from Lansing's Ferry. Conrad Beal."

Case moved into a better position and remained there until the riders were within a hundred yards. They halted. He could verify that it was the marshal just as the lawman raised his arm, palm forward, and called out to Ben.

"Town Marshal Beal, Mister Albright! I got one of your men here with me."

"Come along," said Ben. "But first tell me who those men with you are."

"Posse!" Beal called out as he motioned the men forward. The town marshal rode up first, drew rein, and sat his saddle, looking at the wreckage and the two shiny gun barrels aimed directly at him. He mumbled a profane word and got down heavily from his saddle. "Your man told us about the stampede," he said to Ben. "I thought he was stretchin' things a mite. Now I see he wasn't."

Ruben struggled down to the ground and then hobbled up to Albright. "Did everyone else make it, too, Mister Ben?" he asked.

"We're still waiting on Ferd, but the rest of us made it, Ruben," Albright replied. "And we're mighty glad to see you did."

"Miss Atlanta . . . ?"

"I'm fine, Ruben," came from Albright's niece who was standing up behind the wagon. She smiled at him and his face beamed when he saw her.

"What were these settlers doing when you came onto them?" Ben asked.

"Ridin' up this way, Mister Ben. I told 'em all about the stampede."

Marshal Beal fisted his hands and pushed them deep into his trouser pockets. He stood wide-legged, gazing at Ben Albright but saying nothing. Behind him, his five posse men made no move to dismount. They were keeping close watch upon those two covering gun barrels.

Finally, Beal said: "We come in peace, Mister Albright. I'd feel a sight better if you'd tell them fellows to point those guns in some other direction."

Ben's expression was unrelenting. "I'll tell them nothing," he said. "Ruben told you what happened before dawn this morning. You can see for yourself he didn't exaggerate. Marshal Beal, for all I know those men with you had a hand in this."

Beal remained rooted, his hands still sunk deep in his pockets and his solemn and steady gaze upon Ben Albright. After an interval of standing like this, he nodded his head. "All right. I guess we can't blame you," he growled. "My men been in the saddle a long time though. They'd appreciate gettin' down."

"Bass . . . Case . . . hold off," Ben called out, then he nodded at Beal, and the marshal gave a gruff order. His five riders swung down, being careful to keep their hands well away from their weapons. They stood next to their horses in the scalding sun smash, only their eyes moving.

Beal finally strolled over into the shade of the wagon. He leaned there, still looking grave, still with both hands in his pockets. "Mister Albright," he said, looking down at his boots, "I got to tell you something. He paused, then stated: "Patrick Connelly is dead."

"And who," demanded Ben, "is Patrick Connelly?"

"He was the son of Charles Connelly. Charles

is the mayor of Lansing's Ferry. Mister Albright, Patrick was shot to death while out ridin' his horse some ten miles north of our town." Marshal Beal looked up into Ben's eyes. "You'll recollect Charles," he said. "He was that fellow with the beard who told you Texas drovers weren't welcome at Lansing's Ferry. He was the fellow you argued with about buyin' provisions and gettin' your wagon ferried over the Trinchera."

Ben's hard look remained upon Beal for a long moment of absolute silence. "I know all that. But are you saying . . . ?" He paused before continuing. "Are you saying that in some way I'm responsible for the killing of Patrick Connelly?"

Beal's gaze dropped down again. He seemed both uncomfortable and uncertain. "Mister Albright," he muttered in a voice that carried no farther than to the Texans at the wagon, "it was young Pat who fought one of your cowboys back at the crossin'. Late yesterday mornin' young Pat was found shot through the head. His horse had been shot through the head, too."

Ben, his stare brightening and hardening against Marshal Beal, said: "Just a minute, Marshal Beal. Let me get this straight. I think what you're trying to tell me is that Patrick Connelly's father . . . and some other settlers . . . figured my rider, young Will Johns, slipped back and drygulched Charles Connelly's son, because they had a little scuffle."

Beal inclined his head, but said nothing.

Now Ben's face darkened with fierce color. "So, Charles Connelly rode up here and ambushed my rider. Is that it? And when he decided that wasn't enough to even the score, he caused the stampede."

Marshal Beal still said nothing.

Ben said: "Case, Bass . . . step out here." When both men were standing clear of the wagon, Ben glared at them. "You heard that?" he asked.

"We heard," stated Bass Templeton.

Case Hyle nodded.

"Maybe they killed Ferd, too," Bass pointed out.

"Where is Charles Connelly?" Ben demanded of Marshal Beal.

"I didn't see him after he rode in this morning and told me about young Pat."

"You didn't lock him up?"

Beal looked up. "I didn't know the full of it then," he said. "I only knew his boy'd been shot. He told me that . . . he and the men who were with him who had found young Pat and told Charley."

"And," said Ben, "those men were three in number. Is that right, Marshal?"

"Yes," the lawman answered. "That's right, Mister Albright."

CHAPTER TWELVE

For a long time, there was neither sound nor movement among the men around that wrecked wagon. Sunlight steadily brightened, turning bitterly yellow and scalding. The sky began to fade, to turn brassily pale and sere. On both sides of the Texan camp leery longhorns stepped along to the creek for water.

Atlanta, lingering on the wagon's far side, heard all that was said. She sat down back there, feeling weak, feeling futile. Ruben came around to her there and stood gazing downward. Then he sat down at her side and said: "Easy now, Miss Atlanta. You just rest easy here. Your uncle'll get this thing straightened out. You just see if he don't, ma'am."

The girl settled her anguished eyes upon old Ruben. "How does anyone make a mistaken killing come out right?" she asked.

Ruben fidgeted. He looked far out across the plains, then back to her up-tilted face again. He made a vacant smile and shrugged. He had no answer to this.

Ben Albright, on the other side of the wagon with Marshal Conrad Beal, his posse men from Lansing's Ferry, Case Hyle, and Bass Templeton, made a stony recapitulation, saying: "Connelly found his boy shot to death and thought my rider, Will Johns, had left my drive, gone back, and ambushed his son. And because he thought this, Connelly and three friends stalked us, caught young Will out in the open, and shot him from behind. Is that essentially what it amounts to, Marshal Beal?"

"Near as I can figure," Beal confirmed, "that's about what it amounts to, Mister Albright."

"Do you know Connelly did this? Do you know he shot my rider and caused this stampede that happened before dawn this morning?"

"No," stated Beal, "I don't *know* it. But I think that's what has happened." Beal looked at Ben from troubled eyes. "That's why I brought a posse with me and come out here this mornin' instead of later in the day, after I'd had time to ask around Lansing's Ferry about what happened. I wanted to be here in case there was more trouble." Beal looked around. "I was too late," he said in conclusion, and resumed his melancholy stance.

Ben and Bass Templeton exchanged a long and significant gaze. Feeling like he'd been reasonable long enough, Ben stood up and said: "Marshal, my rider didn't leave this drive for one minute, let alone long enough to ride near twenty miles, shoot a man, and ride back the same twenty miles. Every one of us here knows that to be a fact because Will Johns was never out of our sight."

"Yeah. I figured that, too, Mister Albright," Beal responded to Ben, although he was looking at Bass. "You see, as we rode up here this mornin', we did some spreadin' out as we tracked. We found the prints of those men ridin' south you told me about yesterday. We also found fresher tracks of four men who come together about twelve miles back, then rode up along the creek in the dark and afterward crossed over west of your herd . . . and caused that stampede." Beal paused. "We even found your tracks, being that they were from shod horses, comin' south into town, Mister Albright . . . but we found no other tracks of shod horses, at all. That's why I don't believe your rider went back and bushwhacked Pat Connelly."

"Did his father say my rider did that?"

Beal nodded. "He was bad off. He was all broke up. You got to understand, Mister Albright, young Pat was Charley's only child. He figured the sun rose and set on that lad. He was sort of crazy . . . sort of out of his head . . . when he rushed into my office yesterday. He said a lot of things, but mainly he said it was you Texans who were responsible. I got to admit, Mister Albright, it seemed reasonable to me at the time." Beal stopped and shrugged. He looked at the tough-set faces of Case Hyle and Bass Templeton, before continuing. "That's why I didn't lock him up. I wanted to investigate a little before I went after anyone." He returned his glance to Ben. "I didn't have anything to go on. You understand?"

Ben did not answer. He stared at Marshal Beal with a coldness that never flagged, never diminished. He stepped around him, then halted stiffly to stare over at the corralled horses. He didn't turn around, but said: "I reckon you want me to sit back and take all this."

"I ask you to let me get Connelly my own way," said the lawman.

"What do you want from a man?" Ben yelled wrathfully, turning on the balls of his feet. "I had a good man killed for no reason. Another is missing. I was damned near killed myself, along with my niece and the balance of my crew, Marshal Beal. I've lost possibly a hundred cattle. And you have the guts to ask me to let you handle this your way." Ben raised an arm toward the wagon. "A hundredweight of flour and a ferry trip would have prevented this. Your Charles Connelly's not going to be let off by any damned sodbuster law for this, just because we're Texans and you're Yankees. I give you my word for that, Beal." Ben swung his head. "Case, you and Bass get saddled. Rig out a horse for me, too."

Marshal Beal stood there, dark and unstirring, watching lanky Ben Albright. His discomfort atrophied and was replaced by a rugged cast to his countenance.

"Don't go near Lansing's Ferry," he warned

as he saw a freshening shine to Albright's anger as the Texan glared at him. "The folks are all worked up. They believe your man killed Pat. Charles told them that . . . him and his friends. It'll be suicide if you ride down there, Mister Albright. They'll kill you on sight."

"That," said Bass Templeton, as he moved past toward the rope corral, "is a boot that fits both feet . . . that killing business." He paused to glower back at the five posse men, waiting for one of them to take this up.

None did. They looked from the big Texan to Marshal Beal, shifted their feet as one. The man on the far left raised a shirt sleeve to wipe away the sweat running down his face.

Ruben scuttled around the wagon, peeked at Ben's face, and scuttled back from sight again. Case saw him do this and ignored it. He was watching Marshal Beal. Clearly, the lawman was trying to come up with some way to prevent the Texans from riding into Lansing's Ferry. Counting himself, there were six settlers. Counting Ruben there were four Texans.

Marshal Beal evidently gave up his notion of fighting it out though, for he said to Ben: "Do you know what you're fixin' to do, Mister Albright? There have been two boys killed. At least one of them died by mistake. You go down there now after Connelly . . . and ten, maybe twenty more men are goin' to die. You and your men will be among them. For what? Because a crazed father shot first and didn't reason at all. But you won't be no better if you go to Lansing's Ferry, Mister Albright. So, I'm askin' you . . . please don't go down to Lansing's Ferry. Let me go back and arrest Mayor Connelly. Let me send for a judge advocate from over at Fort Alert. Let's not start the damned war all over again."

"Begging," Bass Templeton said bitterly, "from a damned Yankee." He spat upon the ground, turned, and went stiffly out to get the horses.

Case did not move. He was not yet certain violence would not erupt here.

Ben relaxed a little, some of the high color draining out of his cheeks. In a nearly normal tone he said to Beal: "I sent a man for soldiers from Fort Alert after my rider was killed, Marshal. I reckon they'll be along any time today. I also expect that when you go back to your settlement and say what really happened, your murdering mayor and his three back-shooting friends will light out. I don't aim to let that happen. We're going to look for our man, Ferd, and then we're going to Lansing's Ferry, and if you have those murderers in your jailhouse . . . fine. But if you don't have them there, we'll find that out, too, and I swear to you we'll take care of them for shooting young Will from behind, the way our folks have always taken care of back-shooters."

Ben turned his back and walked away. He was

almost at the rope corral when he stopped, turned back, and ran his hot stare down the off-side of Ruben's wagon to where Atlanta sat. He stood briefly, turning something over in his mind. In the end, though, he did not go to his niece. He called for Ruben to come over to the corral.

Ruben came, moving swiftly, his face working and his eyes unsteady. "Yes, Mister Ben? You want me to . . . ?"

"I want you to stay here with Miss Atlanta."

"Yes sir. Be proud to, Mister Ben."

"Ruben?"

"Sir?"

"I can't talk to her right now. You explain to her . . . this is man's work. It's got to be done this way. You know what I mean. . . ."

"Yes, sir, I know. I'll explain how it is to her. Don't you fret none about that, Mister Ben," he assured his boss. "I'll explain."

"One more thing," said Ben. "When Owen gets back with the soldiers, send him along to Lansing's Ferry. Tell the officer with him what we're doing. Tell them both about the stampede. And, if Ferd comes in while we're gone, make sure they know to tell us."

"Yes, sir. I'll tell the officer that you've gone after Will's murderer."

Ben nodded. He looked over Ruben's shoulder to where Atlanta sat in shimmering shade, saw how the girl was looking straight out over the

142

dancing land, and frowned, his expression turning uneasy about this. "Make her comfortable," he mumbled to Ruben, then went along to where Bass had their horses saddled and rigged out with booted carbines. Here, he was joined by Case Hyle. The three of them stepped up and sat a moment, regarding those motionless posse men and their leader, then Ben led out.

As they rode past the upturned wagon, Ben halted to look at Beal. He said: "Marshal, if you really want to prevent trouble, leave three of your men here at my camp. My niece is here."

Beal pushed up off the wagon and nodded glumly. "I'll do that, sure, and then we'll ride south with you. We can cover more ground in looking for your man if we spread out."

Ben did not reply to this. He sat quietly, watching Beal relegate three of his settlers to guarding the Texan camp.

Ben finally responded: "No thanks, Marshal. We'll ride our own way."

He flagged at Case Hyle and Bass Templeton, leading out southward in a swift lope. Case turned after a little while to look back. Marshal Beal and his companions were slowly walking their mounts, making no effort to overtake the Texans. They seemed spiritless back there, the way they ground along, all loose and slumped in their saddles.

It was now midday with that evil yellow orb

hanging directly overhead and onto the plain. One could see the riding men writhing from its hot lashings. As they moved southward, Ben's Texans continued to encounter Albright steers among the creek-side growth, drinking or standing in weak shade. But no sign of Ferd. They saw the last of these animals where they forded the Trinchera themselves, eastbound over the yonder prairie until the land firmed up again, then southbound toward Lansing's Ferry.

Bass said to Albright: "We don't know where Connelly's place is."

"We'll find it," ground out Ben. "We'll find it, don't worry none about that. And we'll find that bushwhacking Connelly, too."

Case, who had been silent a long time, now interjected: "I think the wise approach would be from over east of town . . . they wouldn't expect us to come from that direction. Otherwise, I'm betting they've got roiled-up homesteaders keeping an eye out and riding all over the place by now."

Ben considered this, threw a look at Case, and nodded. "I think you've done this kind of thing before," he said. "Would that be during the war?"

Case rode stonily along without speaking.

CHAPTER THIRTEEN

They did not approach Lansing's Ferry until late in the day. Sunset was not far off and the land ran red from that lowering, summer-hazed disc hanging a few feet above the earth's far curving. They walked along, three abreast, watching the land change from prairie to plowed plots and shacks. The village itself was still farther along, visible in the shimmering distance as an ugly low blot upon the horizon.

Where a homesteader's sod house appeared half above and half below the ground, for all the world like a huge prairie dog mound, Ben said: "We'll ask at that place ahead where Connelly lives."

Soon they came down into the yard, spied a bent man in soiled clothing working in the shade of a mud barn over some worn-out chain harness, and reined up under his squinted and uneasy gaze.

"We're looking for Charles Connelly's homestead," Ben said, making a statement of this question, then waiting for his answer.

The settler studied each Texan in turn. He put aside the old harness and responded: "Mister, if I was you, I wouldn't go see Connelly right now.

His son's dead and he's all broke up with his grief."

Ben folded both gloved hands across his saddle horn. "Just tell us where he lives," he said. "We'll take our chances, otherwise."

"You don't understand," protested the settler. "You fellows are Texans and Charley says it was Texans who killed his boy."

Ben said nothing to this, but he continued to hold the settler's attention with his steady pale stare as he waited.

Gradually the settler's expression changed. It seemed to crumple as a stirring notion came to him. He licked his lips, lifted one arm, and pointed off to the west. It was very clear now that this man thought Ben and his riders were mixed up some way in the killing of young Patrick Connelly.

"He lives about three miles west o' here. If you cross the north-south stage road into town, then edge a little south, you'll come to his place. It's got a green picket fence around the yard. That's the only painted fence in and around Lansing's Ferry." The settler's arm dropped, his uncertain eyes remaining on Ben. After a brief pause in which he studied Ben's face, he added: "I wouldn't go there, though, if I was you fellows."

Ben turned his horse without a word and led out in a sweeping lope westerly. Case, riding thoughtfully, turned once, far out, and looked back toward that mud barn. The settler was no longer sitting there.

"Gone to get his horse," Ben said aloud, musingly. "No doubt to alert the neighbors we're in the country."

"Let him," swore Bass Templeton. "Let 'em come. Damned if they don't go back a sight faster than they ride out."

Ben said nothing. He was making a straight course for the north-south roadway. After a mile, he slowed to a walk as the road was well in sight.

"Riders," he grunted, and pointed to the south.

Case looked. It appeared to be at least fifteen mounted men. He watched for the reflection of red sunlight off weapons, and saw it. "Armed to the teeth, Ben," he commented. "Just to keep clear we'd best ride north a few miles."

"Run from settlers?" demanded Bass Templeton.

"Call it that if you like," Case shot back. "If they come onto us, we'll never get to Connelly, I can tell you that."

"Case is right," Ben stated, and led them northward in a paralleling way to the distant horsemen.

The yonder riders appeared to be disinterested in three other travelers. Distance made it impossible for them to determine that these were Texans.

Both parties went along for a long hour, then the settlers split off on a westerly course and Ben halted when he observed this.

"Maybe they're bound for our camp," said Bass. "What do you think, Ben?"

"Not likely. But if they are, they won't find anything there but some of their sod-busting friends." Ben swung his horse. "Come on, we've wasted enough time."

There was a series of serrated low land swells west of the Lansing's Ferry roadway. From the eminence of one of these, Lansing's Ferry seemed many miles to the south.

"Didn't have any idea we'd come this far north," commented Bass Templeton. He spat in disgust and squinted onward toward the Trinchera in the direction those other riders had gone. "Hell, they sure made us a heap of extra work."

They passed over several of these up-and-down swales when Case Hyle yanked back and sat still, peering far to his left.

Noticing Case's sudden halt, Ben turned and called: "What is it? What do you see?"

"I'm not sure," Case replied, and reined easterly, riding very slowly and leaning from his saddle. He stopped several hundred yards out, sat for a time in stiff silence, then dismounted and went gingerly forward to halt again, staring down.

"Dammit!" called Ben Albright. "What is it, Case?"

"See for yourself," came back the quick, flat answer. "Ride over here, Ben, and take a look-see."

Case was standing above a dead horse from which the saddle, blanket, and bridle had only recently been removed, leaving tell-tale sweat marks. The earth for yards around had been deeply cut and scarred by dozens of tracks, both man and animal tracks. There were even unmistakable knee imprints in the dust, and the smooth, convex dents made by rifle butts.

Ben and Bass jogged over, stepped down, and stopped dead still to stare, both thinking the same wrenched thought.

Case said quietly: "It's the same horse, Ben. I recognize it. It's the same animal young Connelly was riding when he crashed into Will before the fight."

Bass Templeton leaned a little, pointing. "There's a bullet hole in its head."

Ben went up close and looked hard. Muscles rippled along the edge of his jaw. "It looks like Marshal Beal was telling the truth about this," he said.

Case went closer, also. He knelt on the dead animal's left side and gazed for a long time at the visible bullet hole in the horse's head. After a while he got up and walked carefully around the scene, studying the ground, the area where that tragedy had taken place. Having seen enough, he returned to his horse, mounted, and sat there, still frowning.

Eventually the three of them rode away, south-bound as the curdling dark light strengthened as sunset passed over into early summertime dusk around them.

They breasted the last hill and saw in the middle distance a homestead with its solid log house and log barn.

"This will be Connelly's place," Ben declared, breaking the deep silence that had held all three of them since sighting that head-shot horse.

"And," muttered Templeton, "he won't be there."

"We'll find him," stated Ben. Such was the iron-like timber of his voice when he said this, that Case believed unequivocally that they would find Charles Connelly. Still, he felt instinctively warned as they approached that yard in the gloomy evening.

"Better let me scout ahead," he said to Ben. "That yard is too quiet."

Bass Templeton agreed with this. "By now that settler who directed us here has had more than sufficient time to raise his neighbors. I smell an ambush here, Ben."

Albright drew down to a stop. He moved only his eyes. After scanning the area all around, he said: "All right, Case, go ahead. We'll stay here with your horse."

Case Hyle dismounted, unbuckled his spurs, looped them around the saddle horn, before moving ahead cautiously. The first five hundred feet were covered without incident. The next five hundred put him within close view of the dark buildings and that deathly quiet yard. After that he went along with extreme caution, the warning stronger in his heart.

When he was within a stone's throw of the buildings, advancing inward from the circling east, he dropped flat to skyline the surrounding territory. That was when he caught a brief glimpse of faint light reflected off metal. That one glimpse was enough. He remained quiet and still for a long time. Faint star shine glistened wetly making eerie patterns in the yard. Then, along the barn's rear, he saw an identical faint glitter, and he rose to a stooping stance and began moving back as rapidly as he safely could, until it was safe to get upright.

He went back out to Ben and Bass Templeton, took his reins from Ben, and swung up. "There are armed men in the barn and on both sides of the house. It's an ambush all right."

Templeton swore grittily.

Ben Albright nodded. By this time, it was too dark to see his expression, but his voice was tightly wound and bleak. "All right. Marshal Beal must have got back ahead of us and spread word of our coming. But that won't save Connelly. Now, let's go into town and ask Marshal Beal where Connelly is."

Bass Templeton reared up in his saddle. "That's crazy!" he exploded. "If they got men out here waiting to drygulch us, they'll have three times that many in Lansing's Ferry."

Ben looked round. "You want to go back to camp?" he asked. "That's the only alternative, Bass. We can't sit still. You saw those riders after we left the other homestead. Sooner or later one of those riding bands is going to see us. What do you want to do?"

Templeton was silent. Case, with Ben between them, could sense Templeton's feelings—his indecision and perplexity. Finally, Case said: "All I know is that these here people are too worked up tonight for us to risk riding into their damned village."

Ben lifted his reins. "We won't ride into their village. We'll enter it on foot and from behind Beal's office. Come on."

They skirted wide around the Connelly place, bearing southwest, and sighted no other horsemen in the pre-moon evening until they were close enough to Lansing's Ferry to make out mounted men passing in and out of town on that north-south roadway.

Ben knew this area and led them to an arroyo

that lay a quarter mile west of Lansing's Ferry. He dismounted to lead his horse down into this. Case saw him go ahead a hundred feet, then sink down with a groan, arise, dust his gloved hands, and curse. "They use this gully for a refuse dump," he said irritably, and led off southerly to a spot where there was less litter. Here, they left their horses, passed over the arroyo, and climbed out of it on the far side.

"Stay close and be quiet," said Albright, walking confidently toward the dark bulking backs of buildings. Bass was behind Ben, and Case followed Templeton. In this Indian-file way of going they came to a back alley, and here again Ben stumbled, this time over a broken buggy wheel. He did not swear as he'd done earlier but Case could see a stiffness in his skylined shoulders and knew that he was thinking profane thoughts. Ben paused to study the nearest buildings. He raised a hand, beckoning the others, and started forward again.

Wraith-like, they passed through the faint star light beyond a livery stable, a mercantile establishment that had brine barrels precariously stacked on both sides of a barred back door, and paused just beyond a third building. Set apart from this last building some three or four feet was their destination. Case Hyle, who had never before seen this place from the rear, nevertheless recognized its roofline.

Ben motioned for his companions to remain where they were as he went forward, merging in the dim light with the building's shadows, and remaining in an attentive listening position for a long time before returning to Case and Bass.

"There is someone in there with Beal. I could hear them talking," he told the other two.

"One voice?" Templeton queried.

Ben nodded and motioned with his head. They all moved forward cautiously, halting at the alley-way rear door. Ben rolled fisted knuckles over wood. Case heard those voices go silent. A chair scraped and after that booted feet struck hard upon a plank floor, coming closer.

Case did not see Ben Albright draw his gun because Bass Templeton was between them, but he did see Conrad Beal's face loom clearly in the lamplit door opening. Case saw how Beal looked quickly from Ben's face downward, then up again. Beal's expression said all Case had to know.

"Come in," the lawman said. "You won't need that gun, Mister Albright. I'm alone."

"We heard voices," Ben stated, remaining where he was.

"That was Bill Bodine, a town councilman. He just left."

Ben stepped up into the light, and Case finally saw the gun in his fist. Bass Templeton pushed in and Case followed him. Marshal Beal closed the door. Case whirled to watch this, wanting to be certain Beal did not lock the door. Beal, correctly interpreting Case's look, shrugged and walked on toward his desk.

"I figured you'd come," he told the Texans as he dropped down into the beat-up desk chair.

"Then why have you got posses out hunting us?" queried Ben, still standing, still holding his naked gun.

"They weren't particularly huntin' you," replied Beal. "They've got orders to bring Mayor Connelly in, as well as to prevent you Texans from killin' him . . . if you find him first. That's all."

"Connelly's homestead is crawling with ambushers," growled Bass. "Don't tell us that ain't so, because we saw them out there."

Conrad Beal nodded. He looked tired and worn. "Not to catch you, though. To apprehend Connelly if he returns to his home. There are also guards at his three neighbors' places, too. They've got the same orders." Beal got up, crossed to a little iron stove where a coffee pot simmered, and made a motion toward some tin cups hanging from nails. When none of the Texans accepted this tacit invitation, he poured himself a cup. Walking back toward his desk, he said: "I don't know how Connelly heard I was after him, but he did. When I got back from your camp, he and his runnin' mates were

155

gone. No one seemed to have an inklin' about where they went or what they were up to." Beal drank, put the cup down on his desk top, and sat down in his chair. "I got up some posses and sent 'em after him. Then I waited." He looked straight at Ben. "I figured it wouldn't be a long wait. I knew you three were after him, too. The odds against his gettin' clean away are next to nothin'. But I'm mightily relieved to have you here with me, because now none of my people can say the Texans got Connelly, and that's what's been worryin' me, Mister Albright. If you caught him . . . killed him . . . these here people would always feel like Connelly was some kind of a martyr. That's the point I tried to make up at your camp when I asked you to let me get him my way. I want the settlers to do this thing themselves. That way they'll feel better about it."

"Will they believe he is a murderer?" asked Ben.

Beal arched his brows together over this. "I've passed the word amongst them that he is. I think most of them believed me. I know for a fact the posse men who rode to your camp with me are convinced Connelly is a murderer. They've done their share of talkin', too." Beal sighed. "I think if the settlers catch him, listen to him, see him tried by their own kind of law, and convicted, they'll have no doubts about his guilt, Mister Albright."

"If," said Bass Templeton, "he is convicted."

Beal looked at Bass through an interval of thoughtful silence. Then he said: "Mister, I've sensed how you feel every time we've met. I know why that is, and I won't deny I got some of that same hatred in me, too, like all the rest of us ex-Yankee soldiers here at Lansing's Ferry. But I'm strivin' mighty hard right now to keep that feelin' from influencin' me. I wish you'd do the same, mister, because regardless of Connelly and his kind, we've got to live together here in Texas."

"Why do we have to?" growled Bass.

Beal stood up. His face lost its tiredness, its reasonableness. "Because we're not leaving Texas and neither are you," he flung back at Templeton, his stare smoldering with exhausted patience. "That's why, if we're goin' to live together, we better start actin' like neighbors ought to act. You got any more to say?"

Bass reddened even though he still glared at Beal.

Case Hyle stepped forward, seemingly by accident, interfering with the view these two angry men had of one another. "I'd like to ask you a couple of questions," he said quietly to Conrad Beal. "First off, I'll tell you we saw Patrick Connelly's horse out where it was shot. What I'd like to know now is . . . do you have the gun young Connelly was wearing at the time he was killed?"

Beal gradually relaxed. He looked at Case, still with the smoky glow to his eyes, and nodded. He took a few steps before he turned and sat back down in his chair. He pulled open a desk drawer and took up a six-gun that he offered to Case, butt first. "It's been shot," he said, "if that's what's botherin' you. Pat must've gotten off a couple of rounds at his attacker. I'd guess he got off those shots after his horse fell under him."

Case opened the gate of that pistol, turned the cylinder, saw two spent casings and four unfired cartridges. He handed the gun back to Beal. "One more question. Did Charles Connelly take his son's body home?"

"No. Well, that is . . . he carried it on his saddle horse to his place, then he put it into a wagon and fetched it along to town."

"It's here now?"

Beal nodded, beginning to look puzzled. "Over in the embalmin' shed. Why?"

"Can we see it?"

Beal's puzzlement increased. "What the hell for?" he asked. "It's not very pretty to look at, and no matter what you fellows say, the boy is plumb dead."

"Can we see it, anyway?" reiterated Case.

Beal returned young Connelly's gun to the drawer, closed it, straightened around, and shrugged. "No law against it," he muttered. "Come on." He paused at the door, looked at

Ben Albright, and said in an altered tone: "No gun play. There'll be folks on the walks who'll recognize you Texans. But no arguin' or gun play. All right?"

Ben, who had been looking curiously at Case, finally put up his gun. "If they don't start anything," he told Beal, "neither will we. But, Marshal, it'll be up to you to see that they don't."

Beal opened the door, stood briefly filling the doorway opening, running his assessing gaze up and down the roadway. He turned back to say: "Quiet as a tomb. Come along."

Lansing's Ferry had few pedestrians abroad as the Texans emerged from Marshal Beal's office. The lawman, wise in the ways of his calling, took a circuitous route to the easterly back alley so that even these minimal few settlers caught only glimpses of four men hurrying about in the night. He led them to a combination lean-to, where a top buggy stood, and a ramshackle shed. Here, he led them inside, lit a lamp, and stood back, pointing to a sheeted silhouette upon a dingy table. "That's Pat," he said.

CHAPTER FOURTEEN

Bass Templeton looked disapprovingly as Case went up, removed the sheet, and stood gazing down upon the dead youth. Ben went forward, also. For a full minute they stood there, then Case turned, saying to Marshal Beal: "What did your village doctor say?"

Beal, not looking particularly pleased with this situation, answered: "He told me that there bullet in Pat's temple was what killed him. He also said when Pat's horse fell, he nailed Pat under him breaking both his hips."

Case replaced the sheet, walked to the door, and opened it to pass outside. The others followed him. The four men then returned to Marshal Beal's office. There, Ben Albright stated his determination to resume the search for Charles Connelly. Beal shook his head over this.

"If you do that, Mister Albright, you'll probably not find Charles Connelly and you'll very likely run into one of my posses. Remember, they have orders to stop you, too."

Ben turned toward the rear door. "I'll run that risk, Marshal," he declared.

Beal went along to the rear of his office with the three Texans. There, he opened the door and said: "Mister Albright, if I was you, I'd go back to my camp." As Ben started past, Beal put out a hand to detain him. "The reason I'd do that, Mister Albright, is because although my riders have searched Lansing's Ferry from top to bottom, they haven't found any trace of Connelly, at all." Beal let his hand drop back to his side. "Other riders have combed the land south, east, and west . . . still with no sign of Connelly and his friends."

"That," said Ben sharply, "leaves only the north. Is that what you're telling me, Beal, that you think Connelly may have gone to my camp?"

"He went somewhere, Mister Albright. And he's not anywhere around Lansing's Ferry."

Case pushed past these two older men. He said irritatedly to Bass Templeton: "Come on, dammit. I think Beal's probably right."

Templeton rushed along behind Case. They got back to their mounts a full minute ahead of Ben, were in fact mounting up when Ben came on ordering them to wait. Case ignored this.

He spun up out of the arroyo, loping overland. Bass waited, but impatiently, until Albright was astride, then he too led out northward.

They swept along in a strung-out line, saying nothing to each other until, near the Trinchera, they all came together. Then Ben went toward the creek, exclaiming: "If that damned marshal knew Connelly and his crew were attacking our camp all the time, I'm going to come back here and skin him alive!"

"I don't think he knew that," Bass said, easing his horse over into the water. "I think what he meant was that Connelly must've gone north, because Beal's riders couldn't find him in any other direction."

Case hit the water, roweled his horse, and kept its head downstream. He did not make any attempt to join this back-and-forth conversation. He had his own notion, which was simply that, even if Connelly did attack the Texan camp, Ruben and those three settlers up there would keep him off. What inspired him to hurry though, was a fear that those three posse men Connelly had left at the camp might not wish to fight their own kind, or might be induced by Connelly to leave the Texan camp.

They strung out again, continuing north, after the Trinchera crossing—Case in the lead, Bass Templeton next, and finally Ben Albright, looking grim and determined. They had progressed some two miles from the fording when Case drew rein to let his companions come up. He was sitting twisted in the saddle, looking back. On his right was the creek and its tangled creek-side growth. The moon was now up, slightly fatter than it had been the night before, aiding vision, and behind them lay the broad, silvery sweep of empty plain. Here, where the Trinchera made one of its cutbank bendings, water rushed with purposeful power against an eroded bank making a deep sound.

Bass Templeton, twenty feet east of Case and riding forward, had just raised his head as though to speak, or to see something near the undergrowth, when a slashing burst of rifle flame blossomed a bright red from that direction. Bass's hat sprang away like a frightened bird and his horse gave a tremendous bound, then fell, its rider plummeting limply on a long ten feet, and coming to rest in an awkward heap without moving.

Ben let off a roar and fought his horse around. Case felt the chill breath of a near hit. As he too spun away westward, he drew and fired three times, fast, dumping those bullets into the thicket from where that murderous fire had emanated. It was probably the swiftness of this action that caused the next fusillade to go wide. Although the bullets sang close, neither Ben Albright nor Case Hyle were hit.

They spurred desperately for two hundred yards, then slowed, coming together far out to ride onward another hundred yards before reining down to look back for Bass. Ben's hard breathing was very audible in the abrupt silence.

"They got him," said Ben. "God-damned bush-whackers . . . they got Bass."

Case lit down with his reins in one hand and

his saddle gun in the other. He knelt, dropped two slugs into the far underbrush by shooting high, then waited. There was no response to this fire. Ben came alongside him, also dismounted, his Winchester gripped in his left hand. In that uncertain light, his face was a smooth, deadly mask.

"Hold 'em," he snapped at Case. "Watch for them to break out of there . . . and hold 'em."

Case considered this. They were now only two, their enemies were no doubt greater in number. In addition, they were out upon the exposed plain. He thought of alternatives to Albright's idea but found none he liked, so in the end he nodded agreement.

A solitary, low shot came from over by the creek. It sang past into the pewter night. "Can't see us," muttered Albright. "Shooting in the dark."

Case kept his gaze upon that low-held gun. He had an idea that shot had been discharged to draw return fire so those hidden men could be sure where the Texans were.

He also considered it likely that the gunman, whoever he was, was crawling clear of the brush and creeping forward. There would be no other reason he could accept for that man to be down that low. He settled his elbow upon one knee, snugged back his carbine, and waited.

Two simultaneous shots came at them, one

from the south along the creek and one from the north. Ben Albright nodded over this, saying: "Attempting to flank us, Case. One above and one below us. They'll come out around, if they can."

"All right," Case responded, "that accounts for at least three of them, but are there more?"

Albright made no reply. He settled lower upon the ground, swinging his head far left and far right. The silence ran on, distantly broken by that swift flowing of the cutbank creek. Finally, Ben murmured: "Watch close." Then he half turned to consider the run of prairie to the south. "Like a band of skulking redskins," he muttered. "Or Yankee snipers."

Case waited, widening the scope of his vision until, with that inherent frontier vigilance that was bred into men such as he, the smallest movement stood forth. It was futile to listen for sounds because of the Trinchera's wet rushing, but his steady vigilance was rewarded when a quick winking of dull-toned metal, dead ahead, showed the location where a man was crawling. Case went low over his carbine, concentrating upon that spot.

Far southward and well away from the underbrush a gun flashed. The bullet sang high overhead, and promptly thereafter a second rifleman opened up from the north.

Ben Albright swore with hard feeling. "Like I

thought," he said to Case. "Coming at us from both sides."

Case ignored this, kept his watch for that belly-crawling gunman, and as this settler gently raised up to shoulder his carbine, Case fired. The settler gave a loud scream, sprang high, and went over backward. Ben swung around at this, and elsewhere there were angry cries. Case levered his gun and waited, but that sniper lay without moving, his weapon thirty feet away and thrown there violently by a dying reflex.

Case now placed their encircling enemies, and after a time also located a fourth man. He was behind them!

"Ben, we can't stay here," Case announced. "One of them used the first shots to keep us from guessing what he was up to. Now, I heard a boot strike stone to the west, and that means he's behind us." Case cast loose from his saddle animal. "Come on," he murmured, and led off. Ben Albright followed.

They crawled eastward for several minutes, then halted to listen. The night was deathly still. They crawled on, encountered that sniper Case had shot, and paused beside him only to determine two things—that he was not Charles Connelly and that he was dead. Then they went past, still bearing eastward.

Back where they had abandoned their horses a man's rough voice yelled out in angry disappointment. Case shot Ben a look. "That'll be the one who was sneaking up from the west. From the voice, I'd guess it was Connelly himself."

They loitered a moment, listening for other voices, heard none, and made the last hundred yards to the creek-side undergrowth in a slashing sprint. Ben at once went to the north at the very edge of the thicket, taking the lead now, and then cut west again where Bass Templeton's lumpy form showed faintly against the paler earth.

"Keep a sharp watch," Ben ordered, and passed Case his carbine as he planted himself down beside Templeton, rolled him over gently, and put his head far down. In frank astonishment he looked around, whispering: "By God, he's alive."

Case looked at the unconscious form, put both their carbines into one hand, and reached out for Templeton's shoulder. "Drag him," he hissed at Ben. Together, they retreated a hundred yards back into the undergrowth, hauling Templeton with them. There, clawing deeper into the thicket's thorny security, they made a little clearing and stretched Bass out his full length, face up.

"You keep watch now," said Case, passing the guns to Ben Albright and bending over the disheveled form upon the ground.

Templeton had been struck three times, once

in the left upper arm, again in a curving way across the abdomen and up along his left side, and the third time over the back, up high across his shoulder muscles. None of these injuries seemed to Case likely to prove fatal, which was miraculous he thought, until he recalled that at the time Templeton had been fired upon, he had been riding north and his body had therefore been profiled sideways, not head-on, toward the ambushers. Another factor, no doubt, was that Templeton had been moving when fired at, and the final factor was that the light had not been conducive to good marksmanship.

"How bad?" queried Ben, not looking around, but keeping a tense watch over the faintly lighted plain in every direction.

"He was damned lucky," Case responded. "He's got two muscle shots that don't amount to much, and one up along his side that broke maybe two or three ribs. That one'll pain him, but he'll pull through . . . if . . ."

"If what?"

"If we get out of this alive and back to camp."

Ben made no answer to this.

Case tore Bass's shirt into strips and wrapped his injuries in these makeshift bandages. He then crawled to the creek, filled his hat with water, and crawled back to lessen the injured man's fever. Next, he got his carbine from Ben and stretched out prone, pushing the barrel out.

"I don't like this," mumbled Ben. "It's too quiet."

Case made himself comfortable, saying dryly: "As long as Connelly's after us, at least he's not bothering Atlanta and Ruben."

"How did he come to bushwhack us? How did he know we'd be along?"

"Maybe he heard us coming. I have an idea he was up at the camp, like Beal thought he might be. For some reason he didn't attack, but started back south . . . maybe heard us, and then decided it was a good opportunity to ambush us."

"You're probably right," stated Ben, also getting down flat and peering out past the foremost fringe of underbrush. "He's a damned poor strategist," he said after a while. "An experienced man would never have made it possible for us to get into this thicket, while he and his men went out onto the plain."

Case thought for a minute and then remarked: "He's anxious and he's vengeful. Those things have destroyed a lot of men."

Ben rummaged the yonder night for sound or movement, but there was neither. "What was your rank in the war, Case?" Albright asked Hyle.

"Lieutenant."

"I thought so. You handle yourself like an officer. I was a major. Fourth Texas. You?"

Case lay still. He said nothing, until he felt Ben's gaze fully upon him. Then he said: "Texas

Mounted Rifles, Army of the Cumberland." He turned toward Ben, but could only make out his silhouette as a cloud had passed over the moon.

Ben Albright lay there expressionless, staring back at Case's outline. After a moment, he said very softly: "Army of the Cumberland, Case, was a Yankee outfit."

"That's right, Ben. It was the Fourteenth Corps, then it was called the Fourth Corps, and when the fighting ended, it was known as the Twentieth Corps."

Albright very slowly turned his head away.

Case saw, even in that difficult light, how the muscles along Ben's jaw tightened and rippled. How his visage became darkly stormy. He looked away, putting his somber gaze back out upon the plain again, and thinking how this always came between he and other men. He recalled what he'd said to Atlanta, but he made no attempt to reiterate this same statement to her uncle.

A man's sharp call erupted from the north. Two quick barks answered, one from the south and one dead ahead.

"I guess the waiting is over," ventured Case.

Ben said nothing in response to this.

CHAPTER FIFTEEN

Mayor Charles Connelly had determined where Ben and Case Hyle were by a process of elemental deduction. He verified this by firing into the thicket, then moving swiftly away so that when the return fire came, he was in no great danger. After the skirmish had happened, he collected his men and the three began a stealthy approach toward the creek.

Case had surmised this would be Connelly's maneuver and told Ben. Albright listened carefully, but still he would not look or speak to him. The pair of them lay there in grim silence, waiting. They had been like this for several minutes when Case suddenly raised his head a little, straining toward the north.

"Riders," he said quickly. "Horsemen coming from the north."

At this, Ben raised up. His knuckles were white where he gripped the saddle gun.

Out on the plain there erupted a sharp call. Case knew this was Connelly even though he could not see him. He also knew Connelly had heard this new sound in the night and was warning his companions of it. Case figured about where that voice was, and fired, levered up, and fired again.

An angry burst of mushrooming muzzle blasts came back in response. This was so intense neither Ben nor Case dared raise up off the ground to reply to it. Then that fire storm ceased, a ringing silence settled, and Case cautiously pushed aside some wild grape creepers to peer out. There was no sign of Connelly or his men. He strained, listening for movement, too, and again went unrewarded.

"They've stopped," he said to Ben. "Those riders have stopped out there somewhere. Heard the shooting I expect."

Ben inched forward until he was head and shoulders clear of the thicket. He peered to the north. Case began to push ahead, also, and as he did so, there came the clear sound of several horses rushing all together, heading eastward. They crashed into water, were briefly silent, then emerged upon the Trinchera's far bank and went beating away into the night.

Case sighed, got clear of the underbrush, and stood up. "That was Connelly," he said. "He's run out."

"Get down," growled Ben. "Those other riders are approaching."

Case paused to listen and then turned. He fastened a somber look upon Albright. "That's a familiar sound to me, Ben. That's a troop of Yankee cavalry." He twisted to face the gloomy north, saw a big-hatted civilian scouting ahead, and called out to this recognizable horseman: "Owen, over here in the thicket!"

Ben emerged out of the thicket to stand beside Case just as Owen Wallace rode up and halted. He shot a quick look at Case and Ben, nodded, and turned his horse, calling out: "It's safe this far, Lieutenant!"

"This is a relief," Ben said, releasing a sigh.

Owen Wallace dismounted. "Good to see you, too, Ben. This is our second stroke of luck. We found Ferd on the way into camp. We crossed the creek pretty far north . . . and there he was. His shoulder is dislocated. But he's going to be fine. We left him at camp, along with a few soldiers. We figured you might be heading back, so we decided to head south. Frankly, we were afraid we'd miss you in the dark."

Ben nodded, watched as a dark host of men rode up, stopping five yards out. He watched as one of the men swung down and stepped ahead to where Owen Wallace stood. He touched his hat brim casually.

"Lieutenant Joel Forsythe, U.S. Fourth Cavalry," he introduced himself, and then waited for one of the Texans to speak.

It was Albright who spoke, but his voice was cold. He told Lieutenant Forsythe who he was, explained about the ambush, and about Bass Templeton back in the thicket.

When Ben Albright had finished with his

update, Forsythe informed him: "Mister Albright, your niece is fine. I left a squad there with her. I thought you might be worrying."

Ben made a stiff little nod at this.

"Now, about those men who ambushed you. Did you see them well enough to make a positive identification?"

Ben looked grim. "Only saw one of them up close. He's lying out there where he died." Ben indicated the direction with a flagged flourish of one arm. "But I don't know the man. Never saw him before in my life."

"You shoot him?" the lieutenant asked.

Ben jerked his head sideways. "Mister Hyle there shot him."

Forsythe turned, his face catching the full light of that scimitar moon. He looked at Case for a moment, before saying: "If you'll show my men where your wounded companion is we'll rig out a pack-stretcher and take him back to your camp."

Case nodded, was about to do this when Ben said: "Lieutenant, you take Templeton back to my camp. I'm going down to Lansing's Ferry."

Forsythe was young, but now he looked out at Ben from his youthful blue eyes, and, in a tone that was beyond his years in its assertiveness, said: "Mister Albright, you'll return to your camp with a squad of my men. Mister Hyle will go with me to Lansing's Ferry."

Case did not move as Ben drew up erectly

before that deceptively youthful stare. Both his scarred big hands closed into fists at his sides. He was about to speak when the lieutenant turned his head.

"Sergeant!" he called out.

A battered Irishman appeared from among the dark body of troopers. "Yes, sir!" he snapped out.

"I want this gentleman here . . . Mister Albright . . . to return to the Texan camp with a squad. I want him kept there." Forsythe now put his steady glance back upon Ben. "Those are my orders," he stated. "I will enforce them any way that I must, Mister Albright."

The graying sergeant looked balefully at Ben Albright. He was clearly a long-time veteran, a man with memories, too. He jerked his head at the Texas cowman without speaking, and then looked to Case.

Ben turned abruptly, saying to Case: "I think you will be in appropriate company." Then he walked away.

Forsythe watched Albright go off. Afterward, he said mildly to Case: "What did he mean by that?"

Case shrugged. "It doesn't matter," he answered. "It's a personal thing."

Forsythe, watching Case closely, nodded. "I talked to his niece. I can guess what he meant. I also talked to his old retainer, Ruben Adams.

That's why I ordered him back. I don't want a battle at Lansing's Ferry. My job is to apprehend a killer and ask some questions. Now, about that injured man . . ."

Case led four strapping soldiers to Bass Templeton and stood aside as they carried the wounded man away. He then returned to Lieutenant Forsythe's side, saying: "I have no horse."

Forsythe smiled. "My men picked up two not far from here. They might be even be Mister Albright's. They were spooked by the shooting, I expect." He let his smile die and studied Case a moment before saying: "You've had a rough couple of days. Maybe you'd rather go back with Albright and get some rest."

"I'd rather, yes," answered Case, "but I don't think I will."

Forsythe nodded, called for a horse for Case. When Owen Wallace came up, leading the animal, the officer said to Wallace: "You've done all you had to do. You can go back with Mister Albright."

This was unmistakably an order and Owen's dark face became very still, very antagonistic. He and the young officer exchanged a long look, then Owen turned and walked out where Ben was waiting.

Forsythe nodded at the horse, saying to Case: "Are you ready?"

Case mounted, turned, and led out back to the south and Lansing's Ferry. He rode mechanically, saying nothing, just listening to the soft rustle of leather behind him. Where he led the soldiers across the Trinchera and out upon the east-side bank, Forsythe spurred up beside him to ask a question.

"What did you discover in Lansing's Ferry earlier tonight?"

Case told him all that had transpired. He also told him where Patrick Connelly's dead horse lay, that Marshal Beal had young Connelly's gun, and he concluded by saying Forsythe was prolonging the chase of Charles Connelly by riding along like this and by neglecting to send scouts on ahead to intercept the fleeing men.

Forsythe took this in good part. He called back an order and at once several squads split off from the main company, rushing headlong into the night.

Forsythe lit a cigar as he rode along. He seemed in no hurry, and, although he'd ridden hard for many hours, he did not appear tired. He studied Case Hyle in silence, his interest lively and unconcealed. He obviously would have liked to engage in conversation, but Case's stony profile discouraged this. Finally, he did say: "Why did Connelly think this Will Johns killed his son?"

Case explained how this was. Then, after a pause, he added: "Will couldn't have killed young Connelly. There is plenty of proof that he didn't kill him, too, but Charles Connelly was too blinded by grief to see it."

"What proof, Mister Hyle?"

Case looked around. "Which do you wish to do first . . . catch Charles Connelly, or see the proof?"

"Connelly doesn't worry me," replied the officer. "We'll get him. I've been running down these renegades since the end of the war . . . Reb and Yank alike. My company will get Connelly, so why don't you show me this proof?"

Case changed course, led the soldier company to Patrick Connelly's dead horse, and there, while standing over the animal, pointed to the shot that had killed the beast.

"Take a close look at that wound," he told Forsythe.

After the young officer had dismounted and done this, Case said: "Powder burns, Lieutenant. Did you see them?"

"Yes. The horse was obviously shot from very close quarters. No more than a foot or two away."

Case remounted, waited for Forsythe to get back astride, and, without speaking, resumed riding southward toward Lansing's Ferry. Forsythe caught up to him, looking puzzled.

"Someone shot the horse from close up," he said. "What does that prove, Mister Hyle?"

"I'll show you when we get to the Ferry,"

Case replied, and then remained silent until the company was passing down Lansing's Ferry's main thoroughfare. There, he pointed out Marshal Beal's office, explaining what it was, and that Beal had shown forbearance in the face of Ben Albright's hard truculence. Then, when Lieutenant Forsythe started to rein toward the building, Case stated: "No, not yet. I want to show you the rest of that proof."

He led the officer to the eastward alley behind Lansing's Ferry, and up it to the ramshackle shed behind the doctor's residence. As they neared their destination, the town suddenly came to life despite the late-night hour as word of the soldiers' coming passed rapidly from mouth to mouth.

After the two dismounted, Case led the officer into the shed, pulled out the candle from the door-side bracket, and walked up to the table holding Patrick Connelly's body, where he stopped.

"This," he explained, drawing back the sheet, "is Charles Connelly's son. This corpse is the reason Connelly rode after us, killed young Will Johns from behind, and tried to kill all of us by stampeding the cattle herd over our camp."

Forsythe, hearing the bitterness in Case's tone, looked from Case to the corpse and back again.

"Look at that wound in Connelly's head," ordered Case. "What do you see, Lieutenant?"

"A bullet hole."

Case held the candle low, and waited several seconds before asking: "What else, Lieutenant?"

"Powder burns." Forsythe drew back, looking perplexed. "Powder burns exactly like the horse had. This lad, like his horse, was shot from very close quarters. No more than a foot away." Now the officer straightened and turned fully around toward Case. "Are you inferring that whoever killed this man and his horse was a close friend . . . someone who could approach within a foot or two before killing this man?"

Case moved the candle closer to Connelly's head. He looked upon dead Patrick Connelly without speaking for a while. Then he said, tiredly: "No, that's not what I'm trying to show you at all." He blew out the candle as he walked toward the doorway. "Come along, Lieutenant. Now we can go see Marshal Beal."

Back out in the alleyway filled with soldiers, Forsythe halted Case with an upflung hand. "I don't like mysteries," he said. "I want you to explain this."

Case shook off the hand, went to his mount, and stepped up across it. "No mystery, Lieutenant, but you wanted proof and I'm giving it to you. Come on."

Forsythe motioned for the troopers to follow, then rode on after Case. Where the party of them emerged into the north-south roadway there were dozens of silent, motionless men, some not completely dressed but all round-eyed and hushed, watching the soldiers ride forth, halt before Marshal Beal's office, and dismount. Here, Case waited for Forsythe before entering the building.

Conrad Beal was there at his desk, rubbing both eyes with fisted hands. At the appearance of Case Hyle with a uniformed cavalry officer, he sprang up, both startled and astonished.

"This is Lieutenant Forsythe from Fort Alert," Case announced as he crossed to Beal's desk, drew open a drawer, picked up the six-gun lying there, and handed it to Forsythe. "This is Town Marshal Beal," he concluded, his solemn gaze upon the officer.

Forsythe scarcely looked at Beal. He turned young Connelly's gun over in his hand. He opened the gate, spun the cylinder, smelled the barrel end. He started to say something, but then paused. Very carefully he took the pistol to a lamp and held it up to his face as though to smell the barrel again. He did not move for a full sixty seconds. Then he walked over to an empty chair near the desk and dropped down into it, lifting his wide-open eyes to Case Hyle's face.

"Good Lord. It can't be what I'm thinking, can it?" he asked huskily.

Case reached up to push back his hat. "I don't see how it can be anything else," he replied.

Marshal Beal, alternating his glance from one of them to the other, did not say a word, although it was strongly in his face that he wished to.

Lieutenant Forsythe got up, went back to the table lamp, and made an even closer, more minute examination of young Connelly's fired six-gun.

Beal's office was deathly still. Beyond, in the balmy night, came a murmur of soldier voices. Upon a shelf behind Case a clock ticked rhythmically, and somewhere a long way off a dog bayed at the moon.

Lieutenant Forsythe looked up and across the lamp to Case Hyle. His expression was firmly settled now, knowing and troubled and solemn. He gently put down young Connelly's handgun, drew forth a cigar from an inner pocket, and lighted it by bending to expose the tip over the lamp mantle. Pushing out a gust of smoke, he said to Case: "Who else knows?"

"No one."

"Not the marshal here?"

"Not to my knowledge, he doesn't."

Beal said quickly: "Know what? What's happening here, Lieutenant?"

Forsythe ignored this interruption to ask Case: "Didn't you say anything about this to Albright?"

"No, I wasn't sure. That's why I let you figure it out for yourself. I wanted someone else to come to that same conclusion."

"What?" Marshal Beal snapped loudly, demandingly. "What are you two talking about?"

"Murder," answered Lieutenant Forsythe. "Marshal, we're talking about the absolutely groundless murder of Albright's cowboy, Will Johns."

"How . . . groundless, Lieutenant?"

Forsythe removed his cigar to knock off ash. While doing this, and without looking at Beal, he said: "Are you satisfied this Charles Connelly killed Albright's man? This Will Johns?"

"Yes," answered Beal. "I'm satisfied he did."

Forsythe looked over at Case, held his gaze steadily forward for a long time, then said: "You tell the marshal. You're the one who saw through it first."

Case faced Marshal Beal. "Connelly killed our rider for no reason at all, Marshal Beal. None of us shot his son."

"All right, I believe that. But *someone* shot him, Mister Hyle."

"That's true, Marshal. But he shot *himself!*"

Conrad Beal froze. He blinked his eyes, looking stunned. Finally, he looked over at Lieutenant Forsythe, as though for confirmation of this statement. Forsythe, smoking his cigar, only nodded in agreement.

"Marshal," went on Case Hyle, "young Connelly was riding his horse hell-for-leather out in those swales . . . up one, down the other.

His horse fell. He fell across young Connelly crushing his lower body. You know that. The horse has a broken leg. You can ascertain that yourself by going back out there and having a closer look. Charles Connelly could also have discovered that if he hadn't been out of his head with grief. The horse threshed around. He had young Connelly pinned down. His wild threshing was agony for the boy. Young Connelly drew his six-gun and shot the horse in the back of the head. There are powder burns to prove that."

"I saw the powder burns," breathed Marshal Beal.

"Then young Connelly tried to get out from under his dead horse. He couldn't do it. He discovered that his hips were broken. He may, or may not, have understood that he would never walk again . . . or ride, either.

"Anyway, the agony was more than he could bear. He put the six-gun to his own head and killed himself. He must have known he would more than likely lie out there hidden from sight in that swale indefinitely, in agonizing pain, only to die from his injuries."

Case crossed to the table, took up young Connelly's six-gun, went back, and handed it to Marshal Beal. "Look very closely at the front sight and you'll see, amid the dirt, some horsehair and some tiny flecks of blood."

But Beal did not take the weapon. Instead, he put out a steadying hand to his chair, dropped down, and said exactly the same thing Lieutenant Forsythe had said, and in the same shaken way.

"Good Lord!"

CHAPTER SIXTEEN

A hawk-faced cavalryman entered Marshal Beal's office and threw Lieutenant Forsythe a rough salute. "We've got them cornered, sir," this man reported. "One of them was trying to slip around us in the dark and go north out of the country. We had a cordon out . . . he rode right into it. This one's unhurt. He told us where the other two were . . . at this fellow Connelly's homestead getting fresh horses and some food. We rode there, sir, and threw out a surround. They're still in the barn out there."

"No mistake?" asked Forsythe, putting down his cigar.

The trooper grinned faintly, held up a perforated sleeve, and said: "No mistake, sir."

Forsythe looked at Case and Marshal Beal. "Do you gentlemen wish to come along?" he said in a voice that was quiet and casual.

Case left Beal's office with the officer. As they were getting astride beyond the hitch rail, and Forsythe was giving orders to the soldiers around him, Marshal Beal came out of his office.

He stood there in darkness with lamplight from his opened door silhouetting him from behind. Finally, Beal said: "Lieutenant, I had some men out there watching for Connelly."

The same lanky trooper who had brought news of the surround, said: "With the lieutenant's pardon, I can say to this man that we've got those fellows, too, sir."

"Got them?" queried the officer.

"Yes, sir. We didn't know who they were or whether or not they were friendly, so we put them all in a shed on the grounds there and stationed a guard."

Forsythe smiled. "Come on, Marshal Beal, get your horse. You can tell us if those men are yours or not, and if they are, we'll release them and you can send them home."

Beal went after his horse.

Casually raising his arm, Forsythe spun away and went loping to the north out of town. At his side rode Case Hyle and farther back in squads of four rode the remainder of his cavalry troop. All along the side of the unlit roadway of Lansing's Ferry, men stood like statues, watching this swift exodus. The last rider out of the village was Marshal Conrad Beal, spurring furiously along, trying to catch up.

Case led the way to Connelly's homestead. A mile out he heard gunshots.

At that sound, Forsythe came up to Case, saying: "We'd better go the rest of the way on foot and in skirmish style."

The command halted, orders were given, and at

once several blue-uniformed men appeared to act as horse holders. They took the mounts beyond gun range.

Lieutenant Forsythe drew his revolver, stood close to Case, and said: "I'll advance my men until we contact the other troopers. Then I'll give Connelly a chance to surrender. I hope he doesn't do it."

Case turned to stare. He wanted to say something, but bit his tongue.

Forsythe shrugged. "Think it over," he murmured. "Would you want it on your conscience that you'd killed an innocent man and that your only son was dead by his own hand. Or that you'd nearly killed another man, and that you attempted to stampede a herd of cattle through a camp with the intention of killing other innocent people. And you did all this because you were too hasty in your judgment? I wouldn't, Mister Hyle. I wouldn't want to spend the rest of my life living with a thing like that."

Case watched the officer stride forward, calling out orders that fanned out to the men in his command. An occasional shot came from the dark ahead, and then those dimly seen blue uniforms stepped cautiously and carefully onward.

Case moved with the soldiers, carbine in hand. He had progressed close enough to make out the buildings of Charles Connelly's homestead, when a moving shape materialized at his side. It was Marshal Beal.

"Where's the lieutenant?" he asked breathlessly.

Case pointed in the direction he'd last seen Forsythe. Beal did not move off at once, though. He continued on a little way with Case, commenting to him: "It's unbelievable."

Case settled his eyes on Beal. "Tell that to a young lad named Will Johns, Marshal. I think he'd have trouble agreeing with you."

Where Beal split off to search for Lieutenant Forsythe, Case saw his first winking muzzle blast from the log barn. He kept watching this particular area, wondering which of the renegade settlers was behind that gun, whether he was inside the barn or outside it.

An increasing, flat smashing volley of Springfield carbine gunfire swelled up in the night where Forsythe's men came together, joining with their companions who had maintained the surround. Then they pressed the attack forward and saturated the barn with lead until this deafening clamor reached such a crescendo that Charles Connelly, inside his barn, could not raise up long enough to fire back.

Then the firing stopped abruptly and Forsythe called out to offer Connelly and his companion the privilege of surrender. One solitary shot was Connelly's reply to Forsythe.

Knowing instinctively Connelly himself had

fired that bullet, Case halted to kneel upon the ground. He was certain now that Forsythe had gotten his wish. Charles Connelly was going to fight it out to the flaming end.

Case had no heart for this. It was in his mind that even in wartime he had never encountered a situation where guns and the men who used them were involved in a more pointless, more agonizingly futile fight. Death was in that yonder yard—not heroic or honorable death—only dirty, sordid, mean, and ignorant death.

He stayed on the ground, watching the fight's progress. Maybe five minutes had passed when he saw a blurred shape emerge from the rear of the barn, throw down its carbine, and stand, tense and erect, with both arms high overhead. There was enough moonlight at that moment to make out this man's grimy, thin, and beardless face. It was not Charles Connelly.

Once again orders were passed for the troopers to hold their fire. This time Forsythe's youthful but hard voice directed the surrendering settler to walk away from the barn. This the settler did. When he passed close to the main house, several soldiers stepped out, grabbed him roughly, and faded from sight with their prisoner.

Now there remained only one man in that barn.

Case waited for the volley firing to resume, but it did not.

Instead, Forsythe called into the lull, saying: "Connelly, are you going to come out or not?"

"No!" came back the thundered answer.

"Connelly?"

"Yes."

Forsythe did not answer at once. "Nothing!" he finally called out, biting this one word off. Then he shouted to his men: "Resume firing!"

Case, hearing this exchange and knowing how Forsythe felt, thought he understood why Forsythe had not completed that sentence. Forsythe knew now that Connelly would die in his own yard. He had almost told Connelly how thoroughly, tragically mistaken he had been in all that he'd done, but in the final moment Forsythe had desisted from telling Connelly this. Case could understand Forsythe's gallant reason for this, and agree with it.

It occurred to Case, as the fight was resumed, that Charles Connelly could not hope to cover all the parts of his barn alone. He was wondering when Forsythe would send men to creep in close, when suddenly out in the night the sound of riders behind him, coming up in a stiff trot, made him swing hard around. Just as he did so, those riders stopped somewhere back in the darkness. Case, with a dim suspicion, got up and started walking toward the sound he had heard. Almost immediately he encountered Owen Wallace. They stopped to regard one another, then the swarthy rider came on.

"Slipped off when the guards were bedded down," he said, and made a head wag. "If they'd been Rebs, instead of Yanks, we'd never have got clear."

"Who's with you?"

Owen twisted to look back. "Ben," he said. "There he is."

Ben Albright came up out of the night, stopped to throw a look at Case, before continuing on. The three of them stood quietly for a while, watching that one-sided fight ahead.

Then Ben said: "How did they catch him?"

Case, recognizing that this was said with none of the rancor he'd expected from Albright, recapped the events since leaving Lansing's Ferry, detailing how Connelly had been run to earth.

Ben listened and nodded. "The other one's dead?" he asked.

"One just surrendered. He's with the soldiers. The other one gave himself up, too."

"Only Connelly in that barn?"

"Yes."

Ben stood for a moment without moving, then he said: "Hell, one settler against a whole company of soldiers." He turned and started away, back toward his horse. Case heard him call out: "Ruben, bring those horses back up here!"

Owen Wallace started ahead, lifting and cocking his carbine.

Case said: "Stay out of it, Owen."

Wallace turned. His face was sharp, his eyes bright and shiny. "Hyle, you've given me trouble a couple of times on this drive." He swung the rifle butt savagely upward without another word. Case rolled with this strike, let it graze him, then stepped in, knocking the carbine aside and dropping Wallace with a straight arm punch. He was staring down when Ruben appeared, leading his own horse and one other animal. Ruben sighted Wallace at Case's feet and emitted a quick bleat.

"Is he shot?" Ruben cried. "Is he hurt bad? Case, we got to get him . . ."

"I knocked him out," Case growled, and strolled away, leaving Ruben looking after him, bewildered.

"Gosh darn," snapped Ruben. "A man don't know who is or who isn't his enemy any more. Damn." He knelt to pat Owen Wallace's face to bring him around.

Far ahead, Case encountered Marshal Beal and a bedraggled little crowd of trudging settlers. Beal paused at the sight of Case. They exchanged a long, somber and understanding look, then Case left Beal, walking still closer to the barn.

At that moment, Charles Connelly made a wild rush out of the barn upon a horse. This was a sudden and unexpected attempt for freedom. One moment he was firing from within the barn, and the next moment he was flashing over that ghostly yard, spurring his straining animal madly and firing his handgun as swiftly as he could raise the hammer and tug the trigger.

For several seconds that seemed to Case more like an hour, only Connelly's gun flashed and crashed. In those same seconds Case saw the big, bearded man's twisted face, his moonlighted wild eyes, and his fully open mouth. Then, halfway across the yard, a ragged burst of gunfire dumped Connelly's horse, leaving its rider afoot in a swelling bedlam of flashing weapons.

Connelly stood trading shots as long as his gun would fire. When he was out of bullets, he tried to throw the weapon, but it just fell from his hand as he went down with dust spouting in little bursts from his clothing.

Forsythe was yelling for his men to cease their firing when Case started forward. Silence came, and with it an uncertain, uneasy stillness around the yard. Case got all the way up to the fallen man where he knelt beside him before he detected the solid slap of other booted feet approaching.

Connelly was looking out of fierce but dimming eyes. Case reached for his right arm, which was splayed unnaturally, and placed it upon his chest. He surveyed Connelly's body and saw where a dozen little dark, shiny spots were beginning to appear.

"You put up a good fight," he told the dying man. "Now just lie easy, Connelly. It's all over."

Those fierce eyes, that upturned shaggy face with soft moonglow upon it, began to blur out, to soften away from its fierceness, to assume a peaceful expression. Case took Connelly's left arm and crossed it over the right on his chest. A quiet, long sigh passed Connelly's lips. Then he went still.

Someone standing behind Case struck a match, held it out, perhaps so the group could see the man with whom they had been in battle. But when Case looked up, he realized it was Lieutenant Forsythe, holding an unlit cigar tightly locked between his teeth, hesitating to light it.

As the match flamed out, Forsythe said: "End of the trail, Mister Hyle." Then the lieutenant drew back to call out: "Sergeant Burke, have the horses brought up! Bring along my writing case, too." He paused, then added: "Form up the company!"

Case got up, stepped over Connelly's gun, and moved out into the benign night. He found his horse and was preparing to mount when Ben Albright appeared beside him, already mounted.

Albright waited until Case was astride, then he said: "I sent Owen and Ruben on ahead. You and I will ride back together."

Case said nothing. He turned his horse toward the Trinchera, rode without looking around until he was at the side of the creek, where he waited for Ben to come up. He made a wan little grin before easing into the water, saying: "If I have to cross this creek one more time, I'll have webbed feet."

A mile farther on Ben came up to ride stirrup-to-stirrup. He looked troubled and uncomfortable. "Atlanta told me something you said to her, Case, and I believe it's plumb right . . . about respecting an enemy who fights out of principle. Or something like that. Anyway, that was the idea behind it."

"Ben, that war was over a long time ago," Case stated.

"Yes, it was."

"As long as we will live, won't any of us forget it. I know how you feel, Ben. I saw friends die, too. I also went hungry and shivered in the mud and prayed for the shelling to stop."

They rode all the way back, side-by-side, saying no more.

Within sight of the wrecked camp, they saw that little pencil-thin standing fire, which meant Ruben had a meal cooking. Case drew up, dumped his saddle where it fell, and walked ahead.

Owen Wallace was sitting upon the ground,

drinking coffee. He put a steady gaze upon Case, watched him go where Atlanta stood waiting, and shrugged. A man did things in the heat of excitement that afterward he was ashamed of. As Owen stared into the fire, he had to admit to himself he'd had that punch coming.

Atlanta slipped her fingers into Case's hand to lead him around the wagon. There, still holding onto him, she stopped and pointed at the makeshift bed. Bass Templeton was lying there, washed and freshly bandaged. He and Case exchanged a long look.

They could hear men's voices as Ben Albright and the soldiers and settlers came riding in together to gather at Ruben's fire.

"Glad to see you came through it all in one piece," Templeton said to Case.

"Glad you did, too," responded Case.

"Connelly . . . ?"

"Died in his own yard, Bass."

Templeton let his gaze wander to Atlanta's fingers interlocked with those of Case. He licked his lips. "Some time, when we're alone," he said with slow difficulty, "I'll apologize right for making a damned fool of myself, Case."

"No need, Bass."

"Well . . ."

Atlanta smiled, let go of Case's hand, and dropped down to put her hand on Templeton's arm. She said gently: "Would you like me to bring you some of that stew Ruben is making?"

Bass looked at her a long time before saying in a fading way: "No thanks, Atlanta. I'd just like to sleep a little." He watched them walk away. The thing that was there in his heart finally showed upon his face, but he was alone and no one saw it.

Case let Atlanta lead him far out upon the prairie in the inky darkness where a dip and rise materialized. There she sank down, guiding him next to her with a slight tug of his arm.

"Tell me why it all happened this way," she said.

When he was well launched into an explanation of what had happened since the Albright herd arrived upon the Staked Plains before Lansing's Ferry, she interrupted him, smiling while she said: "No, not that . . . *us*. What made this other thing happen to us, Case?"

He looked at her, wishing he could see her eyes better. It was then that she placed her hand on his cheeks to hold his face, to seek his mouth in the late stillness, and kiss him, and to say, in a wondering tone, afterward: "Would it have happened if we'd met under other circumstances?"

"I have no doubt that no matter where we'd have met," he answered her, "it would have happened. I'm sure of that, Atlanta, but I'm not certain how I know."

"Yes," she said quietly, content with his answer. "I think you are right. No matter where, or how, we'd met, it would have happened this way." Then she smiled at him. "I think perhaps some other way would have been simpler to forget. This never will be."

He put out his hands, let them rest upon her waist. He swayed her to him, holding her close without speaking. He was still holding her this way when the sharp rattle of horsemen approaching camp from the south came to him. He quickly released her to spring up.

"What is it?" she asked breathlessly, getting up to stand at his side.

He listened a moment longer, then took her hand and started forward. "Soldiers," he said. "Lieutenant Forsythe, I imagine. We'd better go back."

"Yes, of course," she said, but she did not look pleased at all.

They returned where a dark mob of men had congregated at Ruben's fire where he was dishing up food and pouring coffee with swift and practiced movements.

Lieutenant Joel Forsythe was standing there, pulling off his gauntlets when Case and Atlanta came up. He put a long, admiring look upon Ben Albright's very handsome niece, and made a little bow. Then he faced Ben, saying: "I'll apologize for returning you to this camp."

Case noticed that he did not say "ordered" you to your camp; his respect for this youthfully deceptive officer went up a notch. Forsythe smiled into Ben's grim expression. He did not appear to be the least perturbed by the stalwart Texan's unfriendly look.

Forsythe continued: "It's always best to apologize after you've stepped on folks' toes, Mister Albright. After one has achieved one's ends." He kept right on smiling. "Anyway . . . it's all over. I have two signed confessions by eyewitnesses . . . Connelly's surviving companions . . . about how your rider was ambushed." Forsythe paused to locate Case. When he had, he said: "Have you told Mister Albright about young Connelly?"

Case shook his head.

"Well," said the officer to Ben, "take a little stroll with me, Mister Albright, and I'll tell you the most unbelievable story you've ever heard . . . every word of which is the gospel truth."

Ben wavered. Ruben, Owen Wallace, and Ferd, with his arm wrapped in a sling, were standing still, watching him, waiting to see if he would walk off with the Yankee officer. Ben looked at the three. He also looked over at Atlanta and Case Hyle, standing close to one another. He joined the lieutenant in a quiet stroll away from the wrecked wagon.

As soon as the two were out of earshot,

Forsythe's cavalrymen, having been smelling the rich aromas coming from the large stew pot, crowded up to the fire where Ruben had remained during the previous conversation.

"Reb," one of the men said, grinning mischievously, "I could sure go for some o' that slumgullion you've got boilin' there. Always did want to see what you fed your soljers to make 'em fight like that."

Ruben glared.

On the far side of him, leaning upon the wagon, Owen Wallace made a very slow, slow smile. "Go ahead and feed them, Ruben. It's probably the onliest he-man cooking this bunch of blue bellies ever got."

Forsythe's grizzled sergeant cocked a dark eye at Owen. These two rugged men took the measure of each other. Then the sergeant's white, heavy teeth showed in a broad smile and everyone except Ruben chuckled.

After a pause, Ruben said: "Humph! Slumgullion! I'll have you know this here is gen-u-wine rabbit stew made from beef. And not just ordinary beef, but real Texas beef!"

One of the soldiers burst out laughing. This was a signal. Everyone laughed, even Case and Atlanta. Over this rollicking sound came a loud call from out on the plain toward the south. Instantly those faces lit by fire light changed to hard sobriety.

The sergeant stepped clear, planted his legs wide, and called back.

He got an immediate answer from out on the prairie. "It's Marshal Beal and some friends from Lansing's Ferry!"

Now Case walked away from Atlanta, went on out a little distance, where he stopped. He heard the steady forward pacing of many horses, sighted a bulky silhouette that he thought must be a wagon, and waited as the newcomers made their approach.

On the seat of a groaning wagon sat Marshal Beal and another man. Around them, riding loosely, were nearly two dozen settler men. Beal, sighting Case, hauled back.

"Brought you a wagon to replace the one that got wrecked," he said. "Got it loaded with salt pork, flour, and dried vegetables." Beal paused to cast an assessing look over the crowd of faces. "Where's Mister Albright?" he asked.

"Here!" boomed Ben, striding up with Lieutenant Forsythe. "Marshal, you didn't have to do that. I'm not exactly a poor man."

"No, I expect you're not," agreed Beal. "But money never was an object in this mess. Anyway, I didn't do it. The folks back at Lansing's Ferry came up with the idea and I just went along." Beal shifted the lines, looped them, before he started to climb down. When he was upon the ground, he said to Ben in a low voice: "It's not any attempt at payment for your rider, Mister Albright. There's no way to undo that. But it is a token of appreciation from the folks of my town to you, for not ridin' down on us like Texans sometimes do, when they're roiled up." Marshal Beal reached out his hand.

Ben looked down at the hand of Conrad Beal. He grasped the man's hand and pumped it once, then let it go, clearing his throat to bellow for Ruben.

"Don't just stand there," he said fiercely. "Get into that there wagon and see what kind of big celebratory meal you can whip up out of it!"

"Yes, sir," responded Ruben, sidling forward. "Yes sir, Mister Ben."

Atlanta squeezed Case's fingers, hard. He turned with her and they went out again, away from that noise of men from whom the last tension had been removed.

A little to one side Lieutenant Forsythe watched them while bringing a cigar forth from a pocket. He did not look down to light this smoke until the night had dimmed out Atlanta's slowly moving figure. Then he sighed audibly, torched up, and turned to find craggy Ben Albright at his side.

Through a cloud of smoke, he said: "Mister Albright, your niece is an uncommonly beautiful girl."

Ben, also looking out where those two strollers had gone, said gravely: Lieutenant, I think she's got uncommonly good taste in men, too . . . even if he was a Yankee."

They turned, those two, and went along to where Ruben, perspiring heavily, was trying to cook and defend himself from a myriad of sly jibes from all sides. They stood together in deep silence for a while, then Ben disappeared around the wagon. He was gone only for a short time. When he returned, he carried two battered tin cups, one of which he handed to Lieutenant Forsythe. He had partially filled the cups with whiskey from Ruben's secret supply. He lifted his cup to the lieutenant.

"To a courageous Union," he said.

Forsythe did not smile when he returned this toast. "Major Albright . . . to a gallant Confederacy."

They drank, and over their shoulders the soft night ran on toward dawn with its sickle moon putting its gentle light over the endlessness of the Staked Plains of Texas.

ABOUT THE AUTHOR

Lauran Paine who, under his own name and various pseudonyms has written over a thousand books, was born in Duluth, Minnesota. His family moved to California when he was at a young age and his apprenticeship as a Western writer came about through the years he spent in the livestock trade, rodeos, and even motion pictures where he served as an extra because of his expert horsemanship in several films starring movie cowboy Johnny Mack Brown. In the late 1930s, Paine trapped wild horses in northern Arizona and even, for a time, worked as a professional farrier. Paine came to know the Old West through the eyes of many who had been born in the 19th Century, and he learned that Western life had been very different from the way it was portrayed on the screen. "I knew men who had killed other men," he later recalled. "But they were the exceptions. Prior to and during the Depression, people were just too busy eking out an existence to indulge in Saturday-night brawls." He served in the U.S. Navy in the Second World War and began writing for Western pulp magazines following his discharge. It is interesting to note that his earliest novels (written under his own name and the pseudonym Mark

Carrel) were published in the British market and he soon had as strong a following in that country as in the United States. Paine's Western fiction is characterized by strong plots, authenticity, an apparently effortless ability to construct situation and character, and a preference for building his stories upon a solid foundation of historical fact. *Adobe Empire* (1956), one of his best novels, is a fictionalized account of the last twenty years in the life of trader William Bent and, in an off-trail way, has a melancholy, bittersweet texture that is not easily forgotten. In later novels like *The White Bird* (1997) and *Cache Cañon* (1998), he showed that the special magic and power of his stories and characters had only matured along with his basic themes of changing times, changing attitudes, learning from experience, respecting Nature, and the yearning for a simpler, more moderate way of life.

Center Point Large Print
600 Brooks Road / PO Box 1
Thorndike, ME 04986-0001 USA

(207) 568-3717

US & Canada:
1 800 929-9108
www.centerpointlargeprint.com